D1478880

REUNION IN SAN JOSE

REUNION IN SAN JOSE

When Robbie Rigg struck gold on his dried-out range, overnight he became a wealthy mine-owner. He could now afford to hire the Lone Star Hellions to find his four runaway children—two wayward sons and two beautiful daughters—and bring them home to San Jose. But five desperate men had guilty secrets—secrets that could be exposed by one of the Rigg boys—if he returned . . .

MARSHALL GROVER

REUNION IN SAN JOSE

Complete and Unabridged

LINFORD
Leicester

First published in Australia in 1984 by
Horwitz Publications,
Australia

First Linford Edition
published April 1987
by arrangement with
Horwitz Group Books Pty Ltd,
Hong Kong

British Library CIP Data

Grover, Marshall
    Reunion in San Jose.—Large print ed.—
Linford western library
I. Title
823[F]   PR9619.3.G7/

ISBN 0-7089-6352-8

Published by
F. A. Thorpe (Publishing) Ltd.
Anstey, Leicestershire
Set by Rowland Phototypesetting Ltd.
Bury St. Edmunds, Suffolk
Printed and bound in Great Britain by
T. J. Press (Padstow) Ltd., Padstow, Cornwall

1

$40 Worth of Dynamite

LARRY VALENTINE and Stretch Emerson reached the sunbaked New Mexico township in the mid-afternoon of an early summer day, their horses slowed down by the heat, their eyes slitted against the sun-glare, scanning San Jose's main stem for their first sight of a saloon; as usual the Lone Star Hellions had a thirst.

Their garb stamped them as ranch-hands, but the locals figured them for would-be prospectors. Nowadays, few strangers arrived in San Jose to seek ranch work. Only three local cattle spreads were still in operation. The town had been founded as a cattle centre, but a gold strike five years before had wrought the inevitable changes. A small army of prospectors worked the foothills of the great mountains to the west and the hilly terrain to the north. San Jose no longer boasted a branch of the Cattlemens Association; the space once occu-

1

pied by that small building now accommodated the double-storied headquarters of the New Era Mineral Company, the biggest of the San Jose mining concerns.

"Sizable burg," Stretch commented. "We could do worse'n hang around a while. Mine towns have been lucky for us."

"And unlucky," countered Larry. "I can recall a mine camp or two that we ought to have ridden around."

"San Jose looks peaceable enough," shrugged Stretch.

The incurable optimist was the taller of the nomads, a gangling beanpole with sandy hair, mild blue eyes, jughandle ears and a ready grin, an easy-going Texan whose scrawny six feet and almost six inches had proved deceptive in a score or more lusty brawls. Stretch was uncommonly strong. And, with the matched Colts slung from his gunbelt, he was ambidexterous. Time and time again he had sided his partner in pitched battles against the forces of lawlessness, though both drifters claimed to be peace-loving, law-abiding and stone-cold determined to mind their own business.

Larry of the nimble wit and questing mentality was some three inches shorter than his towering sidekick, a brawny, dark-haired hombre, passably handsome in a battered, square-jawed way. He packed only one Colt and, like his partner, a Winchester '73 sheathed to his saddle. Though not the complete pessimist, he was apt to tread wary in every new town, to anticipate trouble in one form or another, and not without cause. In the years since the Civil War, these footloose drifters had stumbled in and out of one scrape after another, complaining that none of these fights were of their choosing, but fighting anyway. Trouble was their saddlepard; it clung to them as adhesively as a glued cloak.

As they drew abreast of the McMurtrie & Rusk Mercantile, they were reminded their tobacco-sacks contained little more than a few grains of Durham.

"Might's well buy the makin's," Larry decided, "before we catch up on our drinkin'."

Reining up at the hitch-rail, they dismounted and scanned Main Street and its surroundings and reflected that one New Mexico settlement looked much the same as any other. San Jose's architecture was a mixture of Mexican adobe and American makeshift. Sombreroed and ponchoed peons shared the plank sidewalks

3

with Americanos, some rigged in town clothes, some wearing the rough garb of mine workers. The Texans saw few cowpokes; they might have concluded there were no cattlemen hereabouts, but for the runty buckskin with which Larry's sorrel and Stretch's pinto now shared the hitch-rail.

Studying that animal, noting the set of its saddle and the coiled lariat, Larry grinned wryly and observed,

"At least one cowhand in this territory."

"That's a rancher critter if I ever seen one," nodded Stretch.

They stepped up to the porch and ambled across the threshold, covertly studying the stoop-shouldered old timer at the counter, the store's only other customer and the man who just had to be the owner of that short-backed buckskin hitched out front. He had the look they knew so well, the look of the veteran rancher who had struggled to raise pay-herds for a couple of decades or more of sweat and hardship and bone-wearying toil.

Robbie Rigg was past his prime. Ash-grey hair straggled from under his wreck of a Stetson, matching the drooping mustache that drooped to his sagging jowls. The brown nose was bulbous and slightly tip-tilted and his grey brows shaggy, his cheeks wrinkled like old leather. The polka-dot bandana knotted about his thin neck was sun-faded, like the blue of his rough cotton shirt. The tattered vest sagged like his jowls and his Levis were baggy, tucked into boots that had seen better days. He wore no sidearm. And that figured. How could a man so old, so burnt-out, work up the strength to heft a .45?

Squinting earnestly at the tall, grim-eyed man behind the counter, the old timer mumbled his plea.

"You got my word on it, Mister McMurtrie. Let me have the sticks—just enough to blast the rock away—and there'll be water de-routed from Caballero Creek, nothin' surer. Double R range'll show green again. Purty soon there'll be graze for my cattle and them critters'll fetch a fair price. And then you'll get paid."

"Your word?" McMurtrie was surly, malice showing in his deep-set brown eyes. His clean-shaven visage put the Texans in mind of a buzzard. He was no more prepossessing than the other man, obviously his partner, unloading stock in the south corner of the store. "The word of a no-account who couldn't provide for his own children? There's only you and your woman left at Double R, so how're you gonna carry on—even if you get water for your stock?"

"Old Robbie," drawled the other man. "You try stealin' that creek-water off Bar W land, and Hank Waring's men'll run you and your woman out of the territory."

"You're dead wrong, Mister Rusk." The old man turned to frown at McMurtrie's partner. "It wouldn't be stealin'. I talked it over with Hank and he said go ahead and try dynamite and welcome. He knows it'd take more'n a few sticks to turn all of the creek away from Bar W range." He turned to McMurtrie again. "Just three sticks and a couple feet of fuse."

"No cash. No dynamite." McMurtrie shook his head emphatically. "Your credit's no good, Rigg."

"I done gave you my word . . ." began Robbie.

"I wouldn't take your word—for *anything*," jeered McMurtrie. "And I wouldn't trust any of your whelps—your sassy daughters and your no-good sons."

"Well, hold on now," protested Robbie.

6

"You got no call to talk that way about my boys. What'd they ever do to you?"

"What'd they ever do for you or their mother?" gibed Rusks. "Or for *anybody*?" He quit the corner and came forward to attend the strangers. "What'll it be, boys?"

"Couple sacks of Durham," drawled Larry. He dropped five $10 bills on the counter. "And dynamite. Make it forty dollars worth—and three feet of fuse."

McMurtrie eyed him uncertainly, remarking, "You jaspers don't look like prospectors."

"What d'you want with dynamite?" demanded Rusk. He joined his partner behind the counter, nudged the tobacco to Larry's waiting hand, then made change and looked him over warily. "If you plan on stakin' a claim, you'll need more than dynamite. How're you fixed for pickaxes and spades—supplies . . . ?"

"We ain't prospectors," said Larry. "All we want is the Durham. The dynamite's for this gent."

Robbie's grey brows shot up. Blinking perplexedly at the Texans, he protested,

"You never saw me before—and I ain't beggin' for no handout."

7

"Call it a loan if you want," offered Larry. "You can pay us when you're able."

"No rush," said Stretch, showing the old man an amiable grin.

"You'd stake me?" prodded Robbie. "You'd pay for my dynamite? Why?"

"On account of you need it," shrugged Larry. "And you ain't the first cattleman that ran out of luck and needed help."

"Ranch-hands." Robbie's leather-brown face creased in a pleased grin. "Yup. You're ranch-hands. Takes one to know one."

"Cattlemen got to stick together," opined Stretch.

"Stranger, you'll never get your money back —not a dime of it," warned McMurtrie. "But I ain't a man to discourage trade."

He nodded to Rusk, who retreated to the rear. While the bulky man was fetching the explosives, the old rancher warmly thanked the Texans, offered his name and his hand and insisted he should write some kind of acknow-ledgement.

"Like an IOU," he declared. "Heck, I want for this deal to be set up fair and square."

"We don't need anything on paper," said Larry.

8

"Well, by golly, I ain't about to forget this debt," asserted Robbie. "Listen, how about you boys ride on back to the spread with me? Chloe —that's my wife—she'd be right proud . . ."

"Maybe later," said Larry.

"I don't even know your names," muttered Robbie.

The Texans identified themselves. Rusk came slouching in from the rear room, dumped the dynamite sticks and a small coil of fuse on the counter and, while McMurtrie packaged them, callously predicted,

"The old no-account'll likely blow himself sky-high."

"Don't you fret about me, Lew Rusk," countered Robbie. "Won't be the first time I had to blast for water."

McMurtrie shoved the package at the old man and aimed a derisive grin at the Texans.

"A fool and his money . . ." he began.

"What's your gripe, mister?" Larry voiced his challenge sharply. "How come you talk him down, like he was some kind of deadbeat? He's a cattleman and his luck ran out."

"It's been a long drought," sighed Robbie. "I had a couple hired hands. Had to let 'em go. They got the gold-fever anyway." He shrugged

9

forlornly, picked up his package and made for the entrance. "C'mon, boys. Don't get in no wrangle with McMurtrie on my account."

"These two hombres got their knife in you," muttered Stretch, frowning at the partners. "And my buddy's wonderin' why."

"I got nothin' to say to you," scowled McMurtrie.

"No?" growled Larry. "Well, I got just this to say to you. Next time the old man stops by, treat him respectful."

"We ever hear you talkin' him down again, we're apt to get mad," warned Stretch.

"And that," said Larry, "could cost you a few teeth."

For a moment, McMurtrie and Rusk were tempted to vent their spleen on the strangers. Rusk got as far as clenching his fists. Stretch fixed a cold grin on him and flexed his muscles. With a grimace of impatience, Rusk turned his back. McMurtrie shrugged and said,

"If Rigg never comes in here again, that'll suit me fine."

After a last scathing appraisal of the merchants, the Texans quit the store and followed the old man down to the hitch-rail. Robbie stowed the explosives in his saddlebag and began a speech of thanks, but Larry cut him short.

"Forget it. We'll buy you a drink before you head home."

"Nope." Robbie shook his head firmly. "Already beholden to you boys. Be proud to drink with you, but it won't happen till I can buy the first round." He shook hands with them again. "I ain't about to forget what you done for me. Mind what I told you. Any time you hanker to vist the old Double R, you just saddle up and follow the southeast trail out of town. Chloe and me, we'll be right proud."

Watching the Double R boss ride his runty buckskin along San Jose's main stem, the drifters were reminded of a hundred and one veteran cattlemen they had known and respected. Robbie Rigg was typical of his breed, a work-calloused veteran who would never quit, who would toil while ever he had the strength to sit a saddle, fighting drought, rustlers, anthrax, every kind of set-back bedeviling the cattle fraternity. They didn't feel noble or self-righteous at this moment. Spending part of their combined bankroll to help the veteran out of trouble seemed the natural thing to do.

From the store, they led their mounts across

Main and southward, their destination the Rialto Saloon. They kept their gaze on the painted shingle of that gaudy edifice and thought of whiskey and poker, doggedly ignoring the badge-toter watching them from the porch of the law office.

While Marshal Jeb Noad stared after them, he was joined by the Torrance brothers, Andy and Ed. Many a loner had joined the rush to the San Jose diggings, but so had a great many family men. Of these, the Torrances were typical. Their wives kept house for them in the cabins they had built at the site of their claim. Their children attended the community school. Of squat physique, broad-faced and blunt spoken, the brothers hooked thumbs in their belts and said their piece. Noad, a lean, sad-eyed 40–year-old, shrugged helplessly and tried to meet their challenging gaze, but couldn't.

"Asked you before, Marshal, and now we're askin' again," said Andy Torrance.

"Fair question," frowned Ed. "Is the mayor gonna hire deputies to help you keep the peace —or ain't he?"

"By yourself, you ain't doin' so good," Andy pointed out. "Your father-in-law workin' as your jailer, and him old and feeble."

12

"Too many rowdies in San Jose—and not enough badges," said Ed.

Noad nudged thin fingers into his vest pocket, found half of a cigar and clamped it between his teeth. He spoke quietly and carefully, as though fearful of arousing their ire.

"I reckon you gents know I'm doing my best."

"Nobody's sayin' you don't try," Ed assured him.

"Still doing my best," insisted Noad. "As for deputies—well—I'll remind Mayor Garbutt again."

"If he's frettin' about how much it'll cost, you remind him we got a committee—the Miners Protection League," urged Ed. "We ain't rich, Marshal, not yet we ain't. But we're ready to chip in."

"You tell Al Garbutt," offered Andy. "Tell him, if he'll appoint a couple good deputies, we'll meet him half-way, help pay their wages."

The Torrance brothers went their way and, after another appraisal of the tall strangers hitching their mounts outside the Rialto, Noad retreated into his office.

Business was brisk in the big saloon. When the Texans entered, off-duty miners and townmen were two-deep at the bar and as many more were patronizing the games of chance. They waited their turn to be served, then sampled the local whiskey, rolled and lit cigarettes and watched the winners and losers, the optimists milling about the faro, blackjack and roulette tables. Larry, a poker-player of no mean talent, was impressed by the fact that the Rialto provided no fewer than four tables for that purpose.

"Whoever owns this house, he ain't about to go broke," Stretch opined. "Organized he is. See the bouncer? He packs a shotgun no less."

"I noticed," nodded Larry.

The Rialto was well-protected. Both barkeeps were hefty and muscular, capable of doubling as bouncers. The tablehands were typical of their profession, alert-eyed dealers, dapper, urbane, vigilant. Seated on a dais in the centre of the barroom, a flashily-garbed, easy-grinning jasper cradled a sawn-off shotgun and traded greetings with customers moving back and forth between the gambling tables and the batwings. The Rialto had everything it seemed. Entertainment of a sort was provided by a generously-curved blonde in a figure-hugging gown, strolling among the gamblers and huskily crooning a well-known ballad, to the accompaniment of a lean, cigar-puffing "professor" working hard at an upright piano. The piano was badly in need of tuning and, at that, the blonde woman needed singing lessons, but Larry doubted if the patrons cared a damn; they were too busy ogling her bold figure.

"I'll load a couple plates," offered Stretch, "while you look for an empty chair at one of them poker tables."

"Poker's your game, friend?"

The question was aimed by a portly, well-dressed man who turned to smile at Larry as Stretch drifted away. Double-chinned, prosperous-looking, he sported a diamond stickpin in his flowered cravat. A beaver hat rode rakishly atop his greying dome. He made to offer Larry a cigar. Larry nodded affably and held up his cigarette.

"I play all games of chance," he drawled, "but poker's my favorite."

"Let me introduce myself," said the portly local, offering his hand. "Al Garbutt. Welcome to San Jose, friend. And you can take that as an offical welcome. I happen to be mayor of this town."

Larry shook hands and identified himself, but

won no visible reaction; obviously the Texas Trouble-Shooters were unheard of in this corner of New Mexico. For this he was grateful, having learned that a big reputation could be more trouble than it was worth.

"I'm a personal friend of the owner, Mister Drake Bonner," declared Garbutt, gesturing to the gambling tables, "and I can assure you every game is on the up and up." Noting Larry's travel-stained range clothes, he surmised, "You're itching to risk a month's pay, huh cowboy?"

"For me, it wouldn't have to be a penny-ante game" Larry assured him.

"If you can afford to lose a couple hundred, I think we might accommodate you in one of Drake's private rooms," offered the mayor, nodding to a doorway at the rear. "Easier to concentrate away from the crowds, you know?"

"Sounds okay," shrugged Larry.

The Texans spent an hour in the private poker parlor behind the bar, Stretch watching the play from a corner of the room, Larry playing with his customary skill and steadily losing their entire bankroll—$470. The winners, Drake Bonner, Mayor Garbutt and the house dealer, a pomaded dandy named Cleat

16

Dumont, had won more than mere cash. By sharping Larry, they had won the unrelenting, implacable animosity of a couple of veteran hell-raisers. They would learn, as others had learned, that it didn't pay to gyp the Lone Star nomads.

Drake Bonner, bluff, jovial and handsome, started Larry's blood boiling by jerking a thumb to the door and drawling,

"That's all, Tex. Time for you and your buddy to quit. Better luck next time. Meanwhile, we need the room for other customers."

Larry eyed him coldly, noting his expensive clothes, his gold watch-chain and his paunch— a sure sign of easy affluence.

"I ain't through yet," he growled.

"Said you're cleaned out, didn't you?" grinned Garbutt. "Rough luck, cowboy. I don't reckon Drake'd accept an IOU from a drifter."

"That'll be the day," chuckled Bonner.

"Break out a new deck and I'll take my chances at winning it all back," Larry said bluntly. "I mean a new deck—unmarked." As Bonner and the mayor traded frowns, Larry stared hard at the dealer. "And you, Dumont. No more fast stuff with the hands—savvy?"

The man leaning against the door, a sallow-

17

faced fellow described by Garbutt as Bonner's partner, reached behind him and rapped sharply. He stepped aside and, almost immediately, the door opened to admit the shotgun-toter.

"Now," said Bonner, grinning at Larry. "Say your piece—Mister Sore Loser—but choose your words with care."

"I wouldn't!" snapped the man with the shotgun, leveling his weapon at Stretch.

The taller Texan had risen from his chair. Grim-faced, well aware the shotgun was cocked, he kept his hands clear of his holstered Colts.

"Easy, runt," he cautioned. "It's a set-up."

"As if I didn't know," scowled Larry.

"Careful now, boys," muttered Garbutt. "Let's have no rash accusations here."

"And what was the funny remark about my hands?" challenged Dumont, leering at Larry.

"You know damn well what I mean, you lousy sharper," said Larry. "On that last deal, you fed yourself a couple from under the deck." In cold contempt, he glanced at Bonner and the mayor. "One thing I'll say for you buzzards. You're quite a team. You work slick together —takin' turns to cheat. The saloonkeeper and

18

his hideaway high cards. Garbutt with his signals."

"Do yourself a favor, cowboy," the sallow-faced man sadly advised. "Quit while you still got your health."

"I don't quit till we've played six more hands —with an unmarked deck," declared Larry.

"Whit . . ." began Bonner.

"Yeah, sure," sighed the sallow-faced man. "You don't have to tell me."

He emptied his shoulder-holster and covered Stretch with a short-barreled Smith & Wesson, and Stretch wondered why; he was already covered by the shotgunner. Dumont, grinning derisively, leaned across the table and asserted, "I don't take back-talk from saddletramps— nor sore losers."

Still grinning, he struck Larry with the flat of his hand. Larry, oblivious to the shotgunner, rose up with his bunched left swinging. The butt of the shotgun slammed hard to the side of his head and he was knocked unconscious. But, by then, Dumont was collapsing over his chair, cursing obscenely and bleeding from nose and mouth.

As Stretch made to move forward, he felt the muzzle of the Smith & Wesson rammed into his belly. The sallowfaced man mumbled a warning, but made it sound like a plea.

"Don't make it any rougher on yourself."

Stretch loosed an oath and raised a hand to protect himself, but too late. The man with the shotgun struck out again, chuckling harshly. The butt caught the taller Texan a glancing blow and he went down like a poleaxed steer.

"Usual procedure, Farley," drawled Bonner, yawning boredly. "Invite our trusty marshal to remove the trash."

Nobody had ever asked Farley's given name. All San Jose knew him as Shotgun Farley, and that double-barreled discourager was his most cherished possession.

"Cooled 'em neat, didn't I?" he bragged, as he opened the door. "With this weapon, I can stop a rider at . . ."

"Sure, Farley, sure," grinned the mayor.

"And I never met the man I couldn't put down," declared Farley, "with the barrels or the butt."

"Specially when they can't protect themselves," mumbled the sallow-faced man. "Specially when you clobber them from behind."

"What's *his* beef?" wondered Farley.

"Never mind what Whit says," grinned Bonner. "Go ahead. Fetch Noad." He nodded to Dumont, as Shotgun Farley quit the room. "All right, Cleat. Let's tidy up for the benefit of our gallant peace officer."

Dumont finished mopping at his nose, pocketed his blood-stained handkerchief and gathered up the cards. By the time Jeb Noad arrived, the marked deck had been replaced. Garbutt accorded the lawman a genial grin and offered an explanation.

"Had a little trouble here, Jeb. A sore loser and his sidekick. Do your duty. Stash 'em in a comfortable cell, huh? Give 'em time to cool off, then turn 'em loose. I don't reckon they'll make any more trouble here."

"They claimed they were cheated, Marshal," said Bonner. "So, just so there'll be no misunderstanding, I'll ask you to inspect the deck."

He lit a cigar and gestured to the cards scattered about the table. Whit Marco shrugged resignedly and turned his sallow face to the wall. Noad hesitated a moment, then observed the formality of checking the deck.

"Find any marked cards?" challenged Dumont.

Noad shook his head.

21

"All right, collect their guns," ordered Bonner. "I'll have Farley and a couple of my tablehands tote them to the jailhouse." With a bland grin, he added, "You don't look strong enough to carry them without help."

"As for me . . ." Garbutt rose and consulted his watch, "I've just remembered a previous engagement."

He pocketed his share of the cash, traded winks with Bonner and hustled away. In a matter of minutes, Noad was headed back to his office, followed by four of Bonner's employees, struggling under the weight of the still-unconscious Texans. Dumont returned to the barroom, leaving the owners of the Rialto to talk in private.

"Just once in a while, I wish you'd smile," Bonner chided. "That chest condition of yours —it's not apt to kill you. Doc Mulligan gave you good advice and you ought to heed him. Get more fresh air, Whit. Damnitall, you hardly ever quit the saloon." He grimaced impatiently, as Marco sagged into a chair. "Hell, Whit. With you moping around the place—sad-eyed and pasty-faced—the customers'll be thinking they've stumbled into a funeral parlor."

"If I could forget," muttered Marco. "If I

22

could—wipe that lousy picture from my mind and never remember it . . ."

"What's past is past," Bonner said curtly. "We saw our opportunity and grasped it—and now we're sitting pretty. Give us a couple more years—three at most—and we'll make our fortune here."

"Always so sure, aren't you?" challenged Marco. "Well, just that once, you slipped up. You didn't count on a witness . . ."

"He'll keep his mouth shut," shrugged Bonner. "From us he collects—regularly." He scowled at the tip of his cigar and swore softly. "Don't worry, Whit. He'll never turn us in."

"I almost wish he would," said Marco. "It'd be over then. I'd pay—probably with my life —and maybe I wouldn't mind, Drake. Maybe I'd be better off dead, than living with my guilt."

"You and your guilt," gibed Bonner. "You and your damn-blasted conscience."

"I remember it so clearly—all the time," fretted Marco. "The look in his eyes. He was looking right at me—just before the end . . ."

"Will you, for pity's sake, *forget* it?" snapped Bonner.

"Our kind of luck can't last," warned Marco.

23

"I've stood by and seen you take one sucker after another, here in this room. Always the same routine. Garbutt buttering 'em up, then you and him and Cleat taking them for their last dime."

"No sucker ever tried to hit back at us," asserted Bonner.

"Has to be a first time, Drake," countered Marco. "*This* time, for instance."

"Those saddletramps?" jeered Bonner. "Not a chance. I had 'em pegged right from the start. An easy mark. A couple of no-accounts."

"That's what worries me, Drake," sighed Marco. "You're too confident about everything. I never knew a man so all-fired sure of himself."

"Why don't you help yourself to a bottle, find yourself an empty room and drown your sorrows?" urged Bonner. As Marco shrugged forlornly and got to his feet, he grinned and winked. "But not Ruby's room, huh? I don't hear her singing, and you know what *that* means. She'll be entertaining our friend the mayor."

The Texans came to their senses a few moments after Bonner's men had dumped them in a double cell of the town jail. Larry, the first to rouse, rolled over and stared about him,

24

noting the barred window and door, the two bunks and his horizontal sidekick. He groaned a curse and felt gingerly at his throbbing head, then crawled to where Stretch lay. The taller Texan mumbled incoherently, prised himself up on his elbows and finally mouthed a comment. No longer incoherent, he mouthed every syllable with scrupulous care. And softly, as though fearful a shouted complaint might decapitate him.

"I wouldn't mind the pain of it, if I was hung over from too much booze."

"Me neither," grunted Larry.

"What hurts most," said Stretch, "is the way it happened."

"I think the bouncer clobbered me with his shotgun," mumbled Larry.

"And then he clobbered me—and I couldn't stop him," said Stretch. "On account of the galoot with the pasty face had his gun rammed into my gut." He shook his head and wished he hadn't. Groaning, feeling gingerly at his cranium, he complained, "It wasn't dignified, runt."

"Dignified?" Larry grinned mirthlessly. "No. Not so you'd notice."

"We got took," said Stretch. "They gypped

us just as easily as if we were a couple of lame-brained no-accounts."

"My mistake—lettin' that lard-bellied mayor hustle me into a rigged poker party," acknowledged Larry. He crawled to the nearest bunk, struggled onto it and fumbled for the makings, only to discover his captors had turned out his pockets. "All right. Damn their thievin' souls. I made a fool mistake and it cost us. But they made a mistake!"

"They sure as hell did," agreed Stretch.

He made it to the other bunk, sprawled on it and clasped his hands behind his aching head. The aching had eased, but not much.

"There's a whole lot they don't know about us," muttered Larry.

"Meanin' the mayor, and Bonner and his crooked dealer," said Stretch. "And the hombre with the sick eyes. And the shotgunner."

"What they don't know is you and me got time—all the time in the world," said Larry. "We can afford to watch and wait . . ."

"Stayin' quiet," said Stretch. "Keepin' an eye on them good for nothin' coyotes."

"Lettin' 'em think they got us bluffed," mused Larry. "And then—somehow—I'll figure a way to settle their hash and even the score. And they'll end up sore and sorry."

"Slow and sneaky, huh?" prodded Stretch.

"It'll be a pleasure," growled Larry.

"I can hardly wait," enthused Stretch.

"Yes, you can," countered Larry. "You can wait for as long as it takes. If I can bide my time and stay patient, so can you."

"You know somethin'?" grinned Stretch. "I could damn near feel sorry for them sons of bitches."

The throbbing in their heads had eased somewhat, when Marshal Noad trudged into the jailhouse with his father-in-law in tow. Until this moment, Larry had spared little thought for the San Jose marshal. Now, fixing a jaundiced eye on the badge-toter's solemn visage, he was suddenly interested, and vaguely disturbed. Stretch, who shared his partner's distrust of most lawmen, glanced at Noad and decided against baiting him.

It wasn't that Noad appeared formidable. On the contrary, he wore the yearning, hungry look of a man almost at the end of his tether. His voice was flat, devoid of expression, as he announced,

"You'll be turned loose tomorrow morning.

27

Meantime you might's well take it easy—and forget what happened at the Rialto." He studied them a moment, then turned away. "The jailer will fetch your supper in a little while."

The Texans were silent until they heard the cellblock door clang shut. Then, trading stares with the aged jailer, Larry pensively remarked,

"Your boss is the sorriest lawman I ever laid eyes on."

2

Something Better Than Water

HIS name was Orin Platt, the nervous old timer who had come to San Jose with his son-in-law to stake a claim. He confided in the Texans, though usually reticent with strangers. Bald and bent and shortsighted, his whiskers snowwhite and his movements labored, he was barely adequate for the status of town jailer. Noad had not equipped him with spare keys; too much danger the old man could be lured close to the bars by a prisoner, close enough to be seized. For the same reason, he wore no weapon.

Construing Larry's curiosity as a friendly gesture, he squatted on a stool and answered questions.

"We toiled hard for quite a spell. Didn't find so much as a spoonful of pay-dirt. And Jeb was gettin' desperate. We just had to have cash, had to find some kind of job. So, when the last marshal up and quit, Jeb braced the mayor and asked for his badge."

"Your son-in-law ever tote a badge before?" demanded Larry.

"Couple years back, he was a deputy," frowned the jailer. "But—uh—that was in Kansas. Town called Davoren. A real quiet place."

"You and Noad don't much like it here in San Jose," guessed Stretch. "Too rough for you."

"But we got to stay anyway," mumbled Platt. "The job pays good—and we need cash—need it bad." He bowed his head and confided, "It's on account of my daughter Libby— Jeb's wife. She's been sick the longest time. Her lungs, you know? She's in this sanitarium place couple miles out of Denver, and it costs. Oh, hell . . ." He sighed heavily. "It sure costs. We need every dime we can earn to keep her there. Maybe she'll get better, but we ain't sure. Her only chance, the docs say. If she has a chance at all."

"So Jeb tries to keep the peace," mused Stretch, "in a mighty rough town."

"Doin' the best he can," said Platt. "He don't dare tangle with Mayor Garbutt nor any

30

of the mayor's friends. If we get fired, I don't know how we'll earn enough cash to keep Libby in that Denver hospital. She's a special case, the docs say."

"How's he makin' out?" asked Larry. "As marshal I mean."

"Doin' the best he can," Platt repeated. "Tryin' to please everybody. Tryin' to protect the peace-lovin' townfolks and the miners and their families. Trouble is he can't afford to lean heavy on the wild ones." Blinking uneasily toward the office, he complained, "In this town, you never know how many of them rough jaspers is friends of Drake Bonner."

"We're in this calaboose because your son-in-law has to follow Bonner's orders," Larry said bitterly.

"It'd be Mayor Garbutt gave the order," said Platt. It finally occured to him to ask, "You gents hurt bad?"

"We've been clobbered before, old feller," muttered Stretch. "Takes more'n a sore head to keep us down."

"Jeb checked your horses into the Three Star Livery," offered Platt. "Listen, boys. Uh—when we turn you loose tomorrow—why don't

31

you just ride on out? I mean—if you got cleaned out at the Rialto . . ."

"Sharped," growled Larry. "They took us for our whole bankroll—and we aim to get it back."

"Every last dime," drawled Stretch.

"But you don't have to fret," Larry assured the old man. "Not you nor the marshal. We'll handle it our own way."

"You wouldn't make any trouble . . . ?" began Platt.

"Not for you nor the marshal," promised Larry.

"Well, I'll take your word for that," shrugged Platt, as he rose to his feet. "Only— uh—I keep thinkin' of all that hardware you tote. Three Colts in Jeb's safe. And the rifles. You wouldn't—uh—you wouldn't start a shootout at the Rialto, would you?"

Solemnly the drifters shook their heads.

"We never yet started a shootout—or any other kind of hassle," declared Larry.

"It's always somebody else starts the hassle," explained Stretch. "We're law-abidin', old feller. And peaceable."

"But you plan on squarin' accounts with Bonner," accused Platt.

32

"In our own time—in our own way," said Larry.

"They'll take good care of our animals at the Three Star?" asked Stretch, as Platt began leaving.

"Oh, sure," said Platt. "It's a good enough stable. Mayor Garbutt owns it. He owns every livery in San Jose and a lot of buildings along Main. Must be gettin' rich—real rich—with all them merchants payin' high rents." He paused, scratched at his whiskered jowls and frowned over his shoulder. "I said *he* owns all them places, but I could be wrong."

"Meanin' what?" prodded Larry.

"You know how it is in a town like San Jose —or any other town," shrugged Platt. "A man hears talk. And maybe what I hear is true. It ain't Garbutt owns all that property. It's his wife." He shrugged again. "None of my business anyway. Be back with your supper in a little while."

"Fetch our tobacco," urged Larry. "You got our word we won't set fire to the calaboose."

"To us, a calaboose is like home," declared Stretch.

Left alone, they traded thoughtful stares.

33

"They'll keep," Larry said calmly. "Bonner, the mayor, his sharper-dealer—all of 'em."

"But we'll handle it careful, huh?" guessed Stretch. "Go easy on the marshal?"

"One real sad hombre," mused Larry. "He's got more misery than he can use, so we'll give him a break. When it comes to the showdown, we'll try and keep him out of it."

The Double R ranch-house boasted a parlor but, nowadays, old Robbie and his wife were inclined to eat in the kitchen. They could too easily become depressed and start pining for their children, just the two of them in the room once noisy with the wrangling of their rebellious sons and fiercely independent daughters. Tim Mulligan, the elder of San Jose's physicians, was wont to remark,

"Small wonder the Rigg kids left home. Small wonder they all took off in different directions. Each of them a natural-born rebel and a rugged individualist. Nothing in common with one another, nor with their easy-going parents."

In the past, while calling on the Riggs to tend one of their offspring, the medico had reflected Robbie and Chloe might as well have adopted four strange children and saved Chloe the pain of childbirth. To him, the Double R ranchhouse seemed more a foundling home, so marked was the contrast between the brothers, the sisters, and their parents.

As he seated himself opposite his wife, Robbie wistfully remarked,

"That one well out back gonna save us from dyin' of thirst. Too bad our waterholes couldn't do the same for the herd. Every one of 'em dried out."

"You keep callin' it a herd." Chloe grimaced as she heaped his plate. "All we got is forty head, and none of 'em worth butcherin'."

"Maybe I should've killed us a steer," said Robbie, squinting at his share of the food. "What's this? Beans and greens again—and a few grits? You and me, we're gonna be plumb puny less we get some beef into us."

"Eat it," ordered Chloe. "It'll keep body and soul together."

"For what we're about to receive, make us truly thankful," mumbled Robbie.

"Amen," said Chloe. As she began eating, she sadly remarked, "I'm obliged to the Lord for our vittles, but I wish He'd do more."

"Still pinin' for the young'uns?" frowned Robbie.

"We weren't gonna speak of 'em," she reminded him.

"Let's you and me speak," he shrugged. "Heck, Chloe, they're our kids. I sired 'em and you bore 'em. So who's got a better right to talk about 'em?"

"So I'll say it out straight," declared Chloe. "I'll say I miss 'em and I wish they were back with us."

"I miss 'em just as much," sighed Robbie. He forked up another mouthful, munched and swallowed. "A man ought to have his sons about him, and a mother her daughters."

"It ain't that I'm afeared they can't take care of 'emselves."

"Me neither, Chloe. They'll get by—and then some."

"It's just—it never seemed right, them takin' off the way they did."

"Blame me. I wasn't a good enough provider —couldn't make the old spread pay."

"Not your fault, Robbie Rigg. You did your darnedest and, from the time they were knee-high, Floyd and Mike worked right along with you."

"Till they got discouraged," mumbled

36

Robbie, "and lit out to make their fortune—playin' a lone hand."

"When're you fixin' to use the dynamite?" Chloe demanded.

"Sun-up," said Robbie. "I plan on plantin' the whole bundle deep under the rock-mound —our side of Waring's line-fence. Hopin' the blast'll budge the whole mound and leave a big hollow. If the hollow's deep enough, Waring says I can dig a trench from the near bank of the crick."

"Reckon that'll do it?"

"Reckon so. Water'll run along the trench and into the hollow, fill her up and overflow. Be a littler crick right here on our range. Water enough, Chloe. Purty soon we'll see feed-graze again."

"Soon as we're grazin' a real pay-herd, we send for the kids—that's what you promised," she reminded him.

"We'll send for 'em," nodded Robbie. He finished eating, watched Chloe fill his cup with black coffee, then squinted perplexedly. "How're we gonna send for 'em, if we don't know where they're at? Been quite a spell since any of 'em wrote a letter. Every letter from a

37

different place—and they keep movin' all the time."

"We write to where they used to be," she suggested, "and the postmaster'll send the letters on."

"On to where?" wondered Robbie. "How would they know where they're headed—Floyd or Mike or Belle or Nora—every time they move on?"

"We'll get more letters," Chloe predicted. "Then we'll know how to reach 'em."

Robbie sipped his coffee and grinned wryly.

"You mind the last time we got a letter from Mike? He sent us cash. Proves he's loyal, huh?"

"Fifteen dollars," said Chloe.

"Not much," reflected Robbie. "But it ain't the cash."

"It's the thought," she nodded. "And that's just how I felt when Belle sent us ten dollars from wherever-it-was."

"They're still our flesh and blood," sighed Robbie. "They ain't about to forget their ma and pa."

"Too bad they never favored us," she frowned. "Different as Chinese from Mexicans, as Injuns from Irish, them four. Got nothin' in common with one another."

"'Cept their red hair," he pointed out. "Which they can thank their ma for."

"Not much red left," she complained, raising a work-roughened hand to her ash-grey thatch. "You and me ain't gettin' any younger, Robbie, and that's the pure truth."

"I'm still spry enough to blast for water and raise another pay-herd," he assured her.

After supper, he trudged into the parlor and stared at the framed picture of their children, a photograph taken during the last 4th July celebration before San Jose became a mining town. Gently he lifted it from the wall and toted it to the kitchen. Chloe turned from her stove and, for a long moment, they studied the picture and let the memories flood back.

"Wild they always was—no arguin' about that," he muttered. "But right handsome, huh Chloe?"

"The boys're handsome," she murmured. "The girls . . ." She heaved a sigh. "Just beautiful."

"Like their ma," he grunted.

"Photographer feller grouped 'em just fine," she observed. "Isabelle and Nora standin' side by side. Mike left of Nora with his hand on her shoulder. Floyd right of Isabelle with his hand on her shoulder. Makes it look like our sons are protectin' our daughters."

"And that's kind of funny," said Robbie, "on account of there never was a time them girls needed no protection from Floyd nor Mike. You recall the time the elder Billings boy got a mite too frisky with Nora? Gave him the old one-two, durned if she didn't. Bloodied his ear. Blacked his eye. I don't guess Dave Billings'll ever live it down."

"She'd be all of eighteen now," sighed Chloe.

"Let me think now, that makes Belle twenty-four," Robbie calculated, "her bein' the first."

"Mike's twenty and Floyd's twenty-two," said Chloe. "Old enough to take care of 'emselves—I hope."

"Quit your frettin'," he soothed. "Wherever they are, they're doin' fine."

"But they ain't *together*," she lamented. "They ain't where they ought to be—back here at Double R with their own folks."

"They'll be comin' back," he promised, "just as soon as the old spread can support a growed-up family."

At first light, Robbie saddled his buckskin, stowed his small supply of explosives in a gunnysack and rode west across his parched acres, heading for the rock-mound near the Bar W line-fence. En route, he cast sidelong glances at his surviving stock, forty half-starved steers listlessly fossicking for forrage.

"Stay on your feet," he mumbled. "If I could be this lucky, gettin' enough dynamite to budge the mound, maybe I could talk Holly Soames into sendin' me a couple wagonloads of feed on credit."

Reaching his destination, he ground-hobbled the buckskin a safe distance from the mound, advancing the rest of the way afoot. He burrowed deep at the base of the mound, shoved the bundle in and let the three feet of fuse unwind toward him, then scratched a match. As fast as his legs could move, he hustled back to where the buckskin waited.

Simultaneous with the roar of the explosion, a sizable rock hurtled past him. He jerked to a halt, fell flat and covered his head with his hands. On all sides, the debris showered. His clothing was coated with dust and grit by the time the echo of the blast died away.

Slowly, he struggled to his feet and turned to appraise his handiwork. His first reaction was disappointment. From here, it appeared he had blown away only a third of the mound.

"Needed more sticks," he fretted, as he began trudging back. "Three times as much. But maybe the idea'll still work. Maybe the blast left a deep enough hollow."

For some ten minutes he inspected the gaping hole and the scarred rocks, the jagged edges of the mound and the dislodged boulders. He sank slowly to his knees and pressed his face closer to the scarred rock, squinting intently, feeling the sweat bead on his brown forehead and trickle down his leathery cheeks, knowing his pulse had quickened. His heart seemed to be thumping and heaving as though trying to burst free of his body.

"Easy now," he cautioned himself.

He forced himself to calm, stolidly subduing his excitement. When the clip-clop of hoofbeats reached him, his face was serene. The rider came on slowly, moving across Bar W range, recognizing him and raising a hand in greeting. He returned Vern Dorrington's wave, squatted on a flat rock and waited patiently. Vern Dorrington, the Bar W foreman. Steady kind of feller and a cattleman from way back; one of his own kind. Hank Waring and his craggy-faced ramrod had remained aloof from the hysteria that had gripped the territory after the first gold strike. Bar W was still a working spread, and prospering, thanks to the abundance of graze and water controlled by its owner.

Dorrington reined up, dismounted and, with keen respect for his Levis, carefully climbed the fence.

"Heard the blast," he called. "Been expectin' it. Hank said you figured to buy yourself dynamite."

"Heard it way back to the Bar W ranchhouse?" asked Robbie.

"I was closer," said Dorrington, ambling forward to join him. "Back in the basin in our south quarter. Got a half-dozen men brandin' calves down there." He hunkered beside the old man, stared at the scarred rock for a long moment and said, softly and fervently, "Great day in the mornin'."

"I'm no prospector," said Robbie. "Don't know if you ever prospected, Vern, but maybe you savvy the signs."

"I've—seen quartz before," breathed Dorrington. His hands shook as he delved into his vest pockets for cigars and a box of vestas.

43

Still gaping at the rock-face, he passed a Long
9 to Robbie, slid the other between his teeth
and tried to strike a match, an impossible chore;
he was scratching with the end. Robbie nudged
him. He dropped his gaze to his hands, grimaced and reversed the match. It flared and they
lit up. Puffing a blue cloud, he mumbled, "I
don't know how you can stay so cool, old
Robbie. You savvy what you got here?"

"Looks good, huh?" Robbie grinned mildly.
"Somethin' better'n water."

"All the lousy luck you've had—and now
this," growled Dorrington. "Gold. A fortune I
bet."

"Got to find out for sure," said Robbie.
"And—uh—I don't want no trouble, Vern. I'd
as soon keep it quiet. Don't know how I could
fight off claim-jumpers—gold-thieves and the
like. No use lookin' to Marshal Noad. He's got
his hands full keepin' the peace in the settlement."

"You've always been a good neighbor to
Hank," frowned the ramrod. "I'd say you got
a right to ask favors. Hell, yes. That's puttin'
it mild."

"I was thinkin'—if you could—uh—arrange

44

to send a rider into San Jose," said Robbie, "to fetch the assayer."

"Whoever carries that message, he'll have to be reliable, you know what I mean?" Dorrington nodded vehemently. "I'll choose him careful. A blabbermouth'd spread the news all over town and, next thing you knew, there'd be a wild rush, a riot." He thought it over a moment, then decided, "It better be me. I can keep my lip buttoned when I have to." Abruptly he got to his feet. "Tell you what I'll do. I'll head on back to the ranch-house and tell Hank. You know you can trust him. Then I'll go fetch the assayer—what's his name again? He registers all the gold claims . . ."

"Moran—or somethin' like that," offered Robbie.

"Morgan—Kit Morgan." Dorrington snapped his fingers. "I remember him good. Bought him a beer and listened to him gripe last time I was in town. Claimed he was cheated at the Rialto. Loaded dice."

"I'd take it kindly if you'd fetch him out here," said Robbie. "Quiet-like."

Fortune smiled on Double R that day. There was to be no rush of gold-seekers to the scene of Robbie Rigg's accidental strike, no outcry, no threat to the security of the Rigg spread. By the time Robbie had ridden to the ranch-house, announced the great news and returned to the mound, Vern Dorrington was on his way to San Jose. While the old man hefted his shotgun and kept a wary gaze on the surrounding terrain, the Bar W ramrod rode into the township and made for the assay office.

Morgan, the assayer, was in conversation with a heavyset man in denim pants, alpaca jacket and hightop boots, an angry-eyed fellow who seemed vaguely familiar. They nodded when Dorrington strode into the office, but without interrupting their talk.

"I agree it's a lousy break, Burt," Morgan was saying. "No way to treat a loyal employee."

"I've been supervising the whole operation—right from the time they sank the first shaft," growled the other man. "And now they bring in this Fancy Dan from California—give him my job . . . !"

"I hear tell he's a mining engineer, just like you," said the assayer.

"But no *better* than me . . . !"

"All right, Burt, all right . . ."

"Damnitall, Kit, they've hired him over my

46

head—just because he's a nephew of one of the owners."

"That'll do it every time, Burt. Influence. It isn't *what* you know—it's *who* you know." Morgan turned to eye the cattleman. "Something I can do for you, Vern? You thinking of quitting Bar W and staking a claim?"

"Not me," said Dorrington. "Somebody else."

"I'll see you later, Kit," frowned the other man. "You'll find me at the Lester Hotel, until the end of the week."

"Going back to Colorado?" asked Morgan.

"I'm an engineer, not a prospector." The man shrugged impatiently. "How many mining engineers can San Jose use? There's no other outfit as big as the New Era."

He nodded absently to Dorrington and walked out. The ramrod said his piece then, quietly, but with his eyes agleam with excitement. Morgan listened attentively, then pointed out, as tactfully as he knew how,

"Sounds mighty impressive, friend, but we can't be sure it's what you think. No offense, but old Robbie's no expert."

"I've seen quartz before, and I'm tellin' you the old feller's sittin' on a fortune," declared

47

Dorrington. "And that's why I want you to ride out there with me. Fetch all the documents. Make everything legal for him, so he can't be cheated by bunko steerers or claim jumpers."

"You say he made the strike on his own land?" asked Morgan, rising and reaching for his hat.

"Double R land," nodded Dorrington. "Old Robbie's owned that section since way back when Hank Waring bought all the range west."

"Tell you what," suggested the assayer, as they left the office. "You saw that sorehead I was talking to? That's Burt Kinsell—best mining engineer in the whole territory. Just got fired. He was managing the New Era."

"Yeah, I heard."

"Well now, if your hunch is right, if it's as big a strike as you believe, Rigg's gonna need help. I mean professional help. So maybe Burt'd stay on, at least long enough to get this new claim into operation."

"All right, he can take a look," nodded Dorrington. "Not up to me anyway. If Robbie don't like the looks of him, he'll send him runnin'."

They were headed for Double R a few minutes later, the Bar W ramrod, the assayer

48

and the temporarily unemployed mining engineer. And, by noon, word of the new strike had reached the township and the diggings all across the territory and out by the foothills. There was keen interest, but no great excitement, no fever of anticipation. Morgan and Kinsell confirmed Dorrington's hunch. It wasn't an El Dorado. It wasn't the richest strike Kinsell had ever seen. But Robbie Rigg's days of toil and hardship were over. Kinsell, after checking the indications, compared notes with Morgan; they were mutually agreed it was time Robbie went into the mining business. As Morgan put it,

"Even if this vein peters out in a few months, you'll have made your fortune."

Robbie's reaction was predictable. He rode into San Jose as soon as Kinsell and a couple of diggers had rigged their tents beside the mound. The men were friends of his; he had vouched for them. The owner of the new Double R mine had lingered only long enough to break the good news to his spouse before heading for town to consult Ralph Hodge, manager of the Miners Security Bank. By then, Hodge had been advised of the find by Kit Morgan, who assured him it would be safe to advance funds to Double R; old Robbie could now be considered a good risk.

From the bank, Robbie began seeking the Texans. He took it for granted they would be patronizing San Jose's biggest saloon, so rode along to the Rialto. There, after being congratulated by the owner and staff, he made his enquiry and learned his benefactors had spent the night in the poky.

"Just a little disagreement, Robbie," smiled Bonner. He poured Robbie a shot of bourbon from his private stock and raised his glass in a toast. "You can catch up with 'em later. Meanwhile, we'll drink to your good fortune."

"Mighty sociable of you, Mister Bonner," acknowledged the old man. He sipped his bourbon, smacked his lips and accepted a cigar. "Real Havana, huh? Thank you kindly. It's gonna take me quite a time, gettin' used to good liquor and the best cigars."

"I like to see a deserving case strike it rich," Bonner declared. "You've got it coming, Robbie. Worked hard all your life. Everything comes to he who waits, huh? Well now—you making plans?"

"Oh, sure," grinned Robbie. "First thing I'm gonna do is write a letter. Ain't much for letter writin'. Never had much book-learnin', but I'll find somebody to help me, and then . . ."

"A letter?" prodded Bonner. "You want to get in touch with an old friend—or what?"

"Gonna write to that detective agency, the Pinkerton outfit," said Robbie. "You see, I ain't real sure where my boys are—and Belle and little Nora. Scattered all over. Had no word of 'em in quite a time. Well, this Pinkerton outfit, they're specialists, right? And I can afford to pay 'em, so that's just what I'm gonna do. Hire the Pinkertons to find my young'uns. And then, by golly, we'll be one happy family again."

Whit Marco dawdled across to the table where his partner played host to the old timer. He arrived in time to catch the gist of Robbie's statement, shared a thoughtful glance with Bonner and drew up a chair.

"Robbie—maybe that's not such a good idea," frowned Bonner.

"I don't savvy . . ." began Robbie.

"It's not for me to say," shrugged Bonner. "And I don't mean to pry . . ."

"Help yourself." Robbie grinned cheerfully and took another pull at his drink. "When I'm drinkin' your booze, feel free to pry all you want."

"They've been gone quite a spell, Robbie," said Bonner. "How long has it been—two—three years? It might be too difficult an assignment, even for the Pinkertons. And are you sure you want them back, those wayward youngsters? Where were they when you needed them most?"

"You got it wrong, Mister Bonner," said Robbie. "Ain't no bad feelin' 'tween us Riggs."

"But your children ran out on you," muttered Marco. "Your sons wanted spending money and your daughters craved pretty clothes and the gay life—all the things you couldn't give them."

"That ain't exactly the truth of it," countered Robbie. "Those were hard times out at the old Double R—scarce enough grub to go round. The kids—they didn't want to be a burden to me and Chloe."

"I admire your loyalty," said Bonner. "As for your children, I wouldn't worry about contacting the Pinkertons, if I were you. I remember your boys well—especially Mike . . ."

"Especially Mike," said Marco.

"They can smell an easy dollar a hundred miles away," said Bonner. "It won't be long before they hear of your good fortune, and then they'll be headed home."

"No, I ain't waitin'." Robbie shook his head emphatically. "My mind's set on it. I'm gonna send a letter this very day."

"If you feel that strongly about it, I won't try to talk you out of it," shrugged Bonner. "I'll even draft the letter. The nearest Pinkerton office is in Denver. If we write your letter now, it could reach them tomorrow night." He nodded to Marco. "Fetch pen and paper."

The sallow gambler went up to his partner's office and returned a few moments later, with the writing materials. It took Bonner only ten minutes to dictate the letter, a request that the Denver office of the Pinkerton Agency locate the sons and daughters of Robert and Chloe Rigg. Last known addresses were offered, together with full descriptions of the wayward four. Robbie insisted he could sign his own name, and this proved a laborious chore for him. He thanked the saloonkeeper warmly, after Bonner offered to deliver the letter to the stage depot.

When the old man had gone his way, Bonner grinned wryly at Marco and told him,

"We'll wait a couple days—then give him an answer."

"From the Pinkertons," frowned Marco.

"You can take care of it," shrugged Bonner. "Do I have to spell it out for you? Just a short letter. Sign it anyway you like. The old fool would never recognize your writing. He can hardly read anyway."

Within a few minutes of his quitting the Rialto, Robbie sighted the Texans. They were taking their ease on a sidewalk bench half-way along the block, Stretch boredly whittling, Larry puffing on a thinly-rolled cigarette and staring toward the big saloon. The old man greeted them gleefully, announced his good fortune and was congratulated.

"We're glad for you, old timer," said Larry. "But stay wary, huh? When a man strikes it rich, the coyotes come sniffin'."

"Two-legged coyotes, Robbie," drawled Stretch.

"Ain't nobody gonna sharp me," Robbie assured him. "I got three jaspers on the job already. The assayer'll vouch for 'em, and one of 'em is Kinsell. He's a mine engineer with a big reputation. Whole town knows I made a deal with him, so I don't reckon he'd cheat me." As he repaid the price of the dynamite, he grinned eagerly and suggested, "Let's make it an even fifty—or maybe a couple hundred. Why, I'd still be a dirt-poor rancher with no fortune, if you boys hadn't stopped by the store."

"Forty is all you owe," Larry said firmly. "Forty is all we'll take."

"I hear things," said Robbie. "You boys got cleaned out."

"Our problem—not yours," countered Larry. "Go take care of your claim, old timer."

"All the luck, Robbie," said Stretch.

Repayment of the loan meant a return to solvency for the Lone Star Hellions. At a small bar on South Main they found a dice table and, after assuring themselves the dice were not loaded, decided to risk just $10. By the time they quit the bar, Larry had built that small stake to a useful $80. They could now afford to check into a cheap rooming house and prolong their stay in San Jose.

Early evening, two days later, while they dined at the Crystal Palace Restaurant, the newly-rich Robbie Rigg again sought them out.

3

Find Four Redheads

THE change was drastic, so much so that the rancher-turned-mineowner was accorded an ovation by the proprietor and the other diners. Robbie acknowledged this tribute with a cheerful wave and a good-humored grin, as he made his way to the Texans' table. His new clothes were tailor-made, but not too flashy. Grey pants and a checkered vest, a hammertail coat of black broadcloth, snow-white linen and a string tie and, to top off the tasteful ensemble, a beaver hat.

"Mighty purty," approved Stretch, as the old man seated himself. "You look real dignified, Robbie. Kind of like an undertaker."

"Give me a couple more days, and I'll get used to this new rig," shrugged Robbie. "Chloe's idea."

"How're things at the claim?" asked Larry.

"Just fine," said Robbie. "We'll be ready to

ship our first load to the smelter day after tomorrow. Kinsell and the hired hands, they been workin' like beavers. But—uh—that Kinsell . . ."

"Well?" prodded Larry.

"What he says is right," frowned Robbie. "We had us another parley today. He says, inside a few weeks, he'll be movin' on. You see he offered to get the shaft dug and—uh—give us a start. Well, he'll hold to his end of the deal, but then I'll have to pay him off. And he says I ought to make it a family operation, get my boys home so they can take over."

"Makes sense," shrugged Stretch.

"Yeah, sure. It's what I wanted anyway." Robbie nodded vehemently. "Gettin' rich means only one thing to Chloe and me. The Riggs reunited—all your young'uns back where they belong. But I knew it'd be quite a chore —roundin' 'em up I mean. So I fixed up to send a letter to the Pinkertons . . ."

"You got nothin' to worry about," Larry assured him. "With the Pinkertons on the job, it's only a matter of time."

"Uh—well—that's what the matter is," sighed Robbie. "Pinkertons can't help me."

"Howzat again?" frowned Stretch.

"I got their answer today," said Robbie. "Mister Marco fetched the letter out to the spread and read it to me. Seems they're short of help right now. No men available for the assignment, they say."

"Marco . . . ?" prodded Larry.

"Mister Bonner's partner," explained Robbie. "Him and Mister Bonner was real friendly. Sent my letter to Denver and all."

"It's none of my business, but I'm a mite curious," said Larry. "You want to show me the letter? I mean the answer you got from the Pinkerton Agency."

"I was so all-fired disappointed . . ." Robbie grimaced in disgust. "Tore the damn thing up."

"So now what?" challenged Larry.

The old man talked earnestly and persuasively for the next quarter-hour, describing his children, acknowledging their weaknesses, the fact that his sons were a mite too shiftless and his daughters a mite too ambitious for their own good, the fact that they had quarreled noisily, constantly, from the time they learned to put words together.

"But they're loyal," he emphasized. "Floyd and Mike were always scrappin'. But, if an outsider tried to clobber Mike, he'd have to answer to Floyd. And, if Mike found some galoot beatin' up on Floyd, he'd mix in and help him out. Same with Belle and little Nora."

"All right." Larry nodded slowly. "They struck out on their own . . ."

"Flew the coop," grunted Stretch. "And, by now, they're likely doin' fine."

"But maybe they *ain't* doin' fine," fretted Robbie. "Maybe they're broke and starvin'. How would *I* know? They ain't wrote me in a long time." From under his coat he produced the framed photograph of his offspring. "Here's how they looked three years ago—give or take a month or two. I'm hopin' they ain't changed much. You take the picture with you. And I'll give you cash—plenty cash—for expenses . . ."

"Hold on now . . ." began Larry.

"I trust you boys," declared Robbie. "You find the young'uns, fetch 'em home to the old Double R, and I'll make it worth your trouble. Thousand dollars—what d'you say to that?"

"You want 'em back—even if they don't take kindly to the idea?" frowned Larry.

"I figure I owe 'em," said Robbie. "I was never a good provider. Ain't sayin' it was my fault. Always did my best for 'em, and they knew it. When they up and quit, there wasn't no argument, no hard feelin's. They quit on account of they didn't want to be a burden to Chloe and me. Well, they won't be no burden now. We got cash—more'n we need. I can take care of my kids now. But—first—you got to find 'em."

"You think you owe 'em," mused Larry. "Old timer, *they* owe *you*."

"Yup," agreed Robbie. "They won't be idle, you can bet on that. They'll help run the mine —take some of the load off my shoulders." He grinned wistfully. "And we'll be a real family again."

The Texans thoughtfully studied the picture. Robbie identified his progeny, and Larry noted the sharp contrasts, Floyd lean and handsome, Mike shorter, blocky, blunt-featured, Belle tall and queenly, the tilt of her chin suggesting pride and stubbornness, Nora small and pretty, her smile gentle and guileless.

"Not one of 'em looks like the others," Stretch observed.

"They're red-haired—all four of 'em," offered Robbie. He delved into a pocket. "These are the last letters they wrote to Chloe and me. I don't read so good, but Chloe had two years of schoolin'. She read 'em to me. You keep 'em. Study on 'em. Might help you get started, you know?" From another pocket, he fished a wad of banknotes. "For expenses—five hundred dollars."

Eyeing the money soberly, Larry pointed out, "You scarce know us, Robbie. How come you're trustin' us with a picture of your young'uns—and five hundred dollars?"

"The richer you get, the more careful you ought to be," chided Stretch.

"Happens I mentioned your names to Kinsell," said Robbie. "He's traveled all over, that Kinsell. Worked many a minin' camp. Said he'd heard of you, and more'n once. You the ones they call the Texas Trouble-Shooters?"

"We've been called all kinds of names," shrugged Stretch.

"Kinsell says, if you're the same Larry and Stretch, you'd never take advantage of me," drawled Robbie. "When you boys staked me to forty dollars worth of dynamite, I had you pegged for a couple square shooters."

"Runt, what d'you think?" asked Stretch. "You ain't forgettin' we got a little unfinished business in San Jose?"

"It'll keep," said Larry. "If we're gonna

handle this chore for Robbie, we'd have to come back anyway, when we've found his kids."

"They ain't kids no more," grinned Robbie. He listed the age of each ages of his children. "All growed-up. But I don't reckon they've changed a lot since the photographer-feller made the picture." Studying Larry intently, he recalled, "Kinsell said you used to be a Pinkerton. That a fact?"

Larry shook his head. Stretch explained,

"Pinkerton's wanted to put him on the payroll, but he told 'em no. We don't like to be tied down."

"Well now, how about it?" asked Robbie. "If the Pinkertons wanted you, I guess that proves you got what it takes to find the young'uns and fetch 'em home. We got a deal?"

"We'll do our damnedest for you," said Larry. "I don't know how long it'll take, but we'll keep after 'em until we've found all four."

"Knew I could count on you," declared Robbie, as they sealed the deal with a handshake. "You'll get started rightaway?"

"Maybe tonight," said Larry. "I'll check the letters and look at a map or two. You go on home to Chloe and tell her to quit pinin' for the kids. We'll round 'em up for you, one way or another."

Stretch finished his coffee and watched the old man move out, his step springy, his beaver hat set at a jaunty angle.

"That does it," he warned Larry. "We're in this thing up to our ears. No turnin' back till the job is done. Old Robbie's countin' on us."

"Kirby," said Larry.

"What . . ." frowned Stretch.

"Kirby," Larry repeated. He was noting the addresses on the letters. "Their last letter was from Floyd, writin' from a town called Kirby. That was quite a time back, but it's a start." He pocketed the letters and the cash, donned his hat and tucked the framed photograph under an arm. "Best stop by the Land Office."

"Check a map?"

"You guessed it. Let's go."

They paid their tab and quit the restaurant. The Land Office was closed, but a light glowed from a front window; the agent lived on the premises and was willing to co-operate. It took them less than ten minutes to ascertain that Kirby was located some 180 miles to the northeast.

"Cattle town," offered the land agent. "Well,

63

half-cattle, half-farming. Just a no-account burg. Population about two hundred. You got friends there?"

"Might be," frowned Larry. "We won't know till we get there."

They were gone from San Jose within the hour, packrolls lashed into position, saddlebags filled with provisions, the sorrel and the pinto well rested and their weapons loaded. For the Lone Star Hellions, another quest was beginning. Robbie Rigg had returned to Double R and was assuring his spouse of the Texans' bona fides.

"I got faith in those drifters," he declared. "No matter how long it takes, no matter how far they have to travel, they'll find Floyd and Mike and the girls. All we have to do is pay Kinsell and his men to work the mine, deliver the ore, bank our profits—and wait for our young'uns."

Before quitting town, the old man had stopped by the Rialto to buy a bottle. He saw no need for secrecy where Drake Bonner was concerned; without hesitation he told the saloon-keeper of his deal with the Texans. And then, blissfully unaware of Bonner's chagrin, he started for home.

They gathered in Bonner's office a short time later—Whit Marco, Mayor Garbutt and the storekeepers, McMurtrie and Rusk. Grim-faced and apprehensive, they listened to Bonner's announcement.

"The old man's determined to reunite them —the whole Rigg family. It seems our little scheme with the fake letters didn't discourage him. With money in the bank and his mine in operation, he figures he can buy anything he wants. And, right now, he wants his whelps— back under the family roof."

"You think . . ." McMurtrie licked his lips and squinted nervously. "You think that lousy blackmailer would dare to show his face in San Jose?"

"He'd be tempted, by Godfrey," scowled the mayor. "When he learns of his father's good fortune, he'll get greedy."

"He'll want a piece of the action, nothin' surer," opined Rusk. "Well, damn him to hell, if he comes back . . ."

"Won't be any of us feel safe," said McMurtrie. "He knows too much."

"But would he give us away?" wondered Marco. "Why should he? We've met his demands."

"I reckon I know how his crooked mind works," muttered Bonner. "The moment he's found, the moment he learns about the gold strike on Double R land, he'll start figuring his chances of survival." Coldly, he declared, "There's no doubt in my mind. I *know* what he'll do."

"Always so sure . . ." began Marco.

"Shut up, Whit!" snapped Bonner.

"Just what do you think he'll do?" demanded Rusk.

"Put yourself in his shoes," growled Bonner. "He wants to come home, but home is where his five golden geese are waiting, the five men who've paid for his silence this past two years. It's something he didn't foresee when he left San Jose. The last thing he would have expected—his father finding gold. And now, if he comes home to share in the family fortune, he'll be a target. Any one of us would have shut his mouth long ago, if we'd known where to find him . . ."

"It's what I dream of," breathed McMurtrie.

"Maybe he'll forget what he knows about us," Garbutt suggested. "Let bygones be bygones."

66

"You ready to take such a chance?" challenged Rusk.

The mayor shrugged worriedly, mopping at his sweating brow. Bonner bluntly declared,

"He'll head for the nearest US Marshal's office and tell everything he knows."

McMurtrie and Rusk traded quick glances, while Marco grinned sardonically.

"Hopin' we'll be gone before he gets here?" frowned McMurtrie.

"In custody," nodded Bonner. "He won't feel safe till we're behind bars."

"All right—I guess that settles it," said McMurtrie. "We're gonna have to make sure he never comes back—and never runs to the law. But how?"

"First we have to find him," said Rusk.

"We'll let *them* find him" said Bonner, grinning coldly.

"Them?" prodded Garbutt.

"Old Robbie is paying those saddletramps to back-track his brats," drawled Bonner. "You remember them, the two Texans, the no-accounts we trimmed . . ."

"For a lousy four hundred and seventy dollars," muttered Marco. "I hope you think it was worth the trouble."

"They left town a little while ago, headed northeast," said Bonner. "And maybe they'll get lucky." He chuckled harshly. "Unlucky at cards. Lucky at searching out Robbie's runaway brats."

"Judas goats," mused McMurtrie. "We tag them—let them lead us to the kid . . ."

"The hell we tag 'em," countered Bonner. "I have somebody else in mind for that chore."

"Anybody we know?" prodded Rusk.

"Old sidekick of ours." Bonner grinned at Marco. "Whit remembers him—and knows where to find him. Matter of fact he's holed up not far from here. The old ghost town, Nueva Fortuna. I plan on sending Whit up there tonight."

"Drake's talking about Herb Mathews," Marco told them. "Mathews and his friends pulled a bank robbery in Kansas a couple of months back—or tried to. The thing blew up in their faces. The banker and his cashiers started a shooting match and the local law joined in."

"Mathews and his buddies fled Kansas with a posse snapping at their heels," said Bonner, "and didn't stop running till they found Nueva Fortuna."

"If you can trust these men . . ." began Garbutt.

"They'll handle the chore, if the price is right," said Bonner. "I'll offer them a thousand in advance and another fifteen hundred when the job is done. That's twenty-five hundred, boys. And we all have a stake in the kid's future . . ." Grinning mirthlessly, he amended that statement. "I should say we're interested in making sure the kid has no future—if you get what I mean."

"So we all chip in," frowned McMurtrie.

"Five hundred apiece," said Bonner.

"To get rid of the blackmailer," sighed Marco, "we pay more than he ever demanded."

"Two hundred was the most he ever asked," muttered Garbutt, "from any one of us."

"Call it an investment, Al," grinned Bonner. "The kid dies, and we stop worrying. We keep what we've got."

"The Mathews gang'll follow the Texans," frowned Rusk.

"For as long as it takes them to find the kid," nodded Bonner. "And then—fast and clean—the kid gets his. Exit one blackmailer."

"A money-hungry opportunist," mused

Marco, "who just happened to be in the wrong place at the wrong time."

"*Three* times," scowled McMurtrie.

"I take it we're agreed," said Bonner. "All right, Whit, you can get started rightaway. You ought to make Nueva Fortuna by midnight."

The apparently deserted ghost town was bathed in bright moonlight when Marco idled his hired horse along its broad main street. Tumbleweeds rolled past, propelled by the night-wind. Shutters clattered and loose roof-planks, rotted by the elements, made dull, thudding sounds that started his scalp crawling.

Finding the six desperadoes was no difficult chore. They were occupying the old Fortuna Saloon, their horses stabled out back, a lookout always on duty on the roof, scanning the surrounding terrain. At the sound of a rifle cocking, the gambler hastily identified himself.

"Don't shoot! I'm Whit Marco!"

"Mister, that name don't mean nothin' to me," called the lookout.

"Drake Bonner sent me," Marco announced as he reined up. "Tell Mathews. I've brought a message from Bonner. And money."

A lamp was lit inside the saloon. A gruff voice called to the lookout.

"Fetch him, Shemp."

Moments later, Marco was in conference with six of the most unprepossessing rogues he had ever laid eyes on. And the ugliest of that unsavory half-dozen was the bulky, unshaven Herb Mathews, a flabby, mean-eyed 30–year-old whose paunch sagged over a well-filled cartridge-belt.

Mathews listened to the proposition and, without consulting his cohorts, assured Marco,

"We'll take care of it. Bonner and his pards'll get value for their money."

"It's a chance to shake the dust of this hell-hole off our boots," scowled a hawk-faced man in patched denim. "And that'll suit me fine."

Another man chuckled derisively and remarked,

"Cully's spooked. He claims this burg is haunted. A *real* ghost town."

"It's true, I'm tellin' you," insisted Cully. "I saw it movin' over the rooftops—and it wasn't human. Hell, no."

"How will we know these trackers?" demanded Mathews.

71

"Tall men—well over six feet," said Marco. "Texans. One rides a sorrel, the other a pinto."

"I saw a light east of here," offered the lookout. "Might be a campfire. Might be them."

"So we move out in a little while," decided Mathews. "Find their camp and keep an eye on 'em. Chances are they're the galoots we have to follow." He looked at Marco again. "And this Rigg jasper—the one Bonner's payin' bounty for?"

A nerve twitched at Marco's temple. He bowed his head and spoke huskily.

"There are two brothers. He's the younger. Short and chunky."

"A redhead like the others, huh?" prodded Mathews. "What's his name?"

"I told you the name is Rigg," said Marco.

"His given name," Mathews growled impatiently. "Bonner's payin' plenty to make a corpse of this jasper. I want to be sure there's no mistake."

"There'll be no mistake," sighed Marco. "The elder brother is built lean."

"The name," insisted Mathews.

"Mike." The gambler shrugged resignedly. "The man you have to kill is Mike Rigg."

"I'll take that thousand now," said Mathews. Marco surrendered the money and the other men edged closer, their eyes gleaming. "Don't get any fancy notions, boys. There'll be a divvy-up, but not till the job is done, not till we collect the whole twenty-five hundred. All right, Shemp, Cully, go saddle our horses. Quint and Smitty, you pack our grub—what's left of it. Bannerman, see how much water's in that well. Try and fill every canteen." He pocketed the money and scowled impatiently. "Well? What the hell're you waitin' for?"

While Marco began the return journey to San Jose, the six hard cases traveled east, their destination a clump of cotton-woods. They were camped in the timber by midnight, wrapped in their blankets and cursing the chill of the night air, Mathews having insisted that they build no fire. From the east edge of the copse, Mathews studied the bald ridge some distance away through a telescope, focusing on the glow of the Texans' campfire.

At first light, when the drifters broke camp, Mathews was sure these were the men described by Whit Marco. Their generous height was apparent; they were outlined against the morning sky as they saddled the horses—a sorrel and a pinto.

"It's them, nothin' surer," Mathews reported to his men.

"So," shrugged Cully. "When they move, we move."

"Not all that soon," growled Mathews. "No tellin' how far we'll have to tag these jaspers, so we can afford to take our time."

"No sense tippin' our hand," Shemp conceded.

"I don't crave for 'em to spot us," declared Mathews. "Heed what I'm tellin' you. We're gonna stay out of sight of 'em every mile of the way. Wherever they travel, they'll leave sign. And that's all we need—till they find Mike Rigg."

Kirby had four churches, seven saloons, two banks, a branch of the Cattlemens Association, a scattering of clapboard and adobe cabins accommodating the local citizenry, several livery stables, a surly town marshal and an affable bartender named Wilson. For obvious reasons, including their thirst, the Texans by-passed the marshal's office and put their question to Wilson.

74

It was mid-afternoon of a dry, windless day, the temperature around 95 degrees, perfect conditions for the drinking of cold beer. They propped elbows on the bar of the Snyder & Peck Saloon, put their questions and got their answers. Wilson studied the photograph and grinned good-humoredly.

"Floyd Rigg—sure, I remember him. Nice feller. And good-lookin'." Wilson winked and chuckled. "*Too* good-lookin'—you know what I mean?"

"We don't know what you mean," drawled Larry, lifting his tankard again. "So how about you tell us?"

"Floyd quit town just recent," offered Wilson. "Day before yesterday. He wasn't plannin' on leavin'. It was the marshal's idea."

"He got himself run out of town?" prodded Stretch.

"Three women—includin' the marshal's wife —claimed Floyd was takin' liberties," said Wilson. "He was workin' for Jake Averill, you see. Jake's a carpenter, kind of a general handyman, you know? And he had more chores than he could handle, so he hired Floyd to help out. Floyd's pretty slick with a hammer and saw. He was gettin' along just fine, fixin'

75

windows and busted furniture, stuff like that. Cuttin' shingles for a roof—any old chore—Floyd could handle it."

"He was triflin' with married women?" challenged Larry.

Wilson glanced to right and left, then crooked a finger. The Texans leaned closer and, in a hoarse whisper, he confided an opinion.

"More likely those lyin' females gave Floyd the come-on—you know what I mean? And he didn't want no trouble, so he shied off. Well, they didn't take kindly to that, so they turned mean. First Hannah Dreyfus, then that skinny Phoebe Jessup, and then the marshal's wife."

"No chance they were tellin' the truth?" asked Larry.

"Listen, Floyd's a mighty handsome feller," muttered the barkeep. "Damn near every woman in Kirby had her eye on him, and I ain't sayin' he didn't flirt with a girl or two. But he wouldn't be fool enough to spark some other jasper's wife. Plain truth is those harpies were throwin' 'emselves at him—and he wouldn't play."

"Day before yesterday, runt," mused Stretch. "We ain't far behind him. Might catch up with him soon."

"Depends how far he traveled—and how fast," said Larry. He dropped a coin on the bar and ordered refills, inviting Wilson to draw one for himself. "So the marshal ran him out of town. You happen to notice whichaway he rode?"

"He was headed north," said Wilson. "Might've made for the mountains and Santa Fé. Maybe cut east for Soldado Peak, after he reached the fork. That's five miles north of town."

From Kirby, the Texans followed the north trail for five miles. They were undecided when they reached the fork, the main trail winding on toward the Sangre de Cristos, the other cutting away to the east. But for their encounter with a trio of town-bound cowhands, their decision route might have been decided on the flip of a dime.

One of the cowhands rememberd Floyd Rigg.

"Met him right here couple days ago," he told the Texans. "We talked some before he rode on. Seems he bought himself a mess of trouble in Kirby." He grinned and winked. "Ol' Heart-Breaker Floyd."

"He rode on north?" asked Larry.

"East," said the cowhand. "Said he'd try his

luck at Soldado Peak. Might be safer for him there, come to think of it. Not many women at the Peak."

The cowhand and his buddies resumed their ride to Kirby, while the Texans took to the east trail.

"Should've asked 'em how far to the Peak," said Stretch.

"Makes no never-mind," grunted Larry. "The Peak is where we're headed, no matter how far."

Grouped atop a rise some distance from the fork, Herb Mathews and his cronies shielded their eyes against the sunhaze and followed the movements of the horsemen, the three heading south, the two riding the east trail.

"They didn't stay long in Kirby," complained Shemp. "Hell, don't they ever get weary, them Texans?"

"They're bein' paid to find the Riggs. Looks like they ain't wastin' no time." Mathews shrugged nonchalantly. "We should complain? The sooner they find Mike Rigg, the sooner we finish our chore—and collect."

After passing a signpost in the late morning, Larry and Stretch ruled against a noon-camp. By keeping their mounts to a steady clip and forgetting their hunger, they could make Soldado Peak before dark.

They were saddlesore and thirsty, their range rig wearing several layers of alkali dust, when they sighted the sprawling township nestling in the shadow of the lofty peak. It was the hour before sundown. And, a few moments after they entered the main stem, they knew they would be spared the need to ask questions; their search for Floyd Rigg had ended.

Half-way along the second block, a curious crowd had gathered. Voices were raised in anger. The marshal of Soldado Peak, long past his prime and obviously intimidated by the shouted abuse of four angry townmen, was vainly trying to restore order. On the sidewalk, two young women watched what promised to become a free-for-all. One of the girls appeared apprehensive, the other giggled in eager antici-pation. The angry towners, young and burly, mouthed threats at a slim redhead who just had to be Floyd Rigg.

The Texans recognized him rightaway, and his accusers used his name, cinching the iden-tification. He stood a shade under 6 feet and wore Levis and a broadcloth jacket that had seen better days. His Stetson was shoved to the back of his head, revealing his generous mane of fire-red hair and a handsome face creased in a troubled frown. He was edging close to a saddled sorrel and attempting to remonstrate with his accusers. He wore no sidearm, but a rifle was sheathed to the sorrel's saddle. Studying him with keen interest, Larry saw little resemblance to the humble, easy-going Robbie Rigg. This lean 22–year-old had gotten himself into another jam, but appeared more indignant than scared.

"You heard what he said, boys," frowned the aged lawman, as the Texans reined up and dismounted. "He's quittin' town rightaway, so what can you win by beatin' him up?"

"He's quittin' town sore and sorry!" one of the men asserted. "He was playin' fast and loose with my wife—and he ain't gonna get away with it!"

"Easy now, George . . ." chided the marshal.

"All I did was tip my hat and say howdy," growled Floyd. "Doggone it, is that a crime in this man's town?"

"I saw you with your hands on my fiancee!" yelled another man.

"Now, Rufe . . ." began the marshal.

"You butt outa this!" snapped Rufe. "We know how to take care of his kind!"

The younger woman giggled again. Floyd scowled at her, then at Rufe, and asked,

"What kind of a jackass are you anyway? I helped the lady cross the street—took her arm like a gentleman should. You got no call to make crazy accusations."

"You was pawin' her! I seen you!" accused the third man.

"We had you pegged for a womanizer, right from the start," declared the fourth man.

"I ain't gonna listen to any more of this," Floyd said curtly. "I haven't been in this town long enough to fool with any woman, and I don't plan on stayin'. A man could get lynched in Soldado Peak—just for *lookin'* at a woman."

"We ain't through with you, mister!" snarled George, advancing with his fists bunched.

"Now—uh—wait on, George . . ." pleaded the marshal.

"Outa my way!" raged George.

He planted a hand against the lawman's chest and shoved, sending him reeling. The older locals mumbled protests, but gave Floyd's would-be assailants a wide berth. Floyd turned to mount the sorrel as the four barged toward him, but changed his mind and stood his ground. Whirling, raising his fists, he scowled defiantly,

"All right, you crazy hotheads! I'll take a lickin'—but not before one of you feels my fist!"

As he strode forward with Stretch in tow, Larry unholstered his Colt and won a brief pause by discharging it to the sky. The roar of the report froze George and his buddies in their tracks. All eyes switched to the strangers. Larry holstered his Colt and said his piece, still moving forward, not stopping until he stood between Floyd and the belligerent four. Stretch came on unhurriedly, grinning amiably at the townfolk.

"Let's not go off half-cocked, boys," advised Larry, eyeing George sternly. "If the redhead was leavin' anyway, you don't need to fret for your women. Back off now."

"Four of you gangin' up on just one hombre." Stretch shook a long forefinger. "For shame."

"Listen, you don't have to buy in on my account," Floyd assured them.

"We're in, like it or not," retorted Larry, without taking his eyes off the four. "Fork your cayuse and make tracks, Floyd. Nobody's gonna stop you."

"You—know me?" frowned Floyd.

"Time enough later for talk," said Larry. "Do like I said."

"The hell with it," growled Floyd. "I don't run from the likes of them."

"Are we gonna let these drifters stand in our way?" George shouted at his cronies. "C'mon! Let's take 'em!"

The marshal called another reprimand, but the hotheads weren't listening. They hurled themselves at Floyd and the Texans, while the onlookers retreated to safe vantagepoints.

4

Almost a Bride

THE marshal of Soldado Peak dusted himself off and backed toward the opposite sidewalk, wondering if he should hustle down to his office and fetch a shotgun; he could think of no other way of checking what promised to become a prolonged riot. By the time he reached the sidewalk, the hassle was under way with a vengeance. But, eyeing the brawlers, he changed his mind about fetching a shotgun. It was all too obvious this ruckus would be short-lived; already the bumptious George was out of the fight, spreadeagled in the dust and breathing heavily.

George was Larry's first victim. His wild swing had missed. Larry's had not. And now, while the elder townmen cheered excitedly and their womenfolk screamed in agitation, Rufe and the other hostiles traded blows with the Texans and got the worst of it.

Squaring off at Stretch, Rufe landed a right

84

to the face, a left to the belly and another right to the side of the head. He might have been a 5–year-old child patting at Stretch with open hands for all the damage he caused; the taller Texan budged not an inch. His only retaliation was a left jab to Rufe's jaw, a short, power-charged blow that drove Rufe off the street and up to the sidewalk to collapse in a store entrance.

Floyd was wrestling the third man when, suddenly his assailant was carried away, seized bodily by Stretch and toted to a water-trough. To the accompaniment of his victim's irate yells and a resounding splash, Stretch dunked him.

The fourth scooped up a fistful of dust and flung it into Larry's face, but Larry was more than ready for that dirty tactic. He barged forward, ducking low under the hail of dust and grit and ramming his bunched right into the man's midriff. He followed that with a lusty uppercut that lifted the last bumptious buck and threw him sideways across the trough where his crony floundered.

It had lasted exactly 2½ minutes. Now, it was over—and then some. George was coming to his senses, but slowly. Rufe lurched to his feet, only to collapse again. The third man struggled to rise from the trough. He couldn't, because his unconscious cohort still hung across it.

The towners accorded the Texans warm applause. Stretch doffed his Stetson to the ladies, while Larry nodded reassuringly to the marshal and announced,

"The redhead won't cause no more trouble. He's comin' with us."

"Who says so?" demanded Floyd.

"I say so," growled Larry.

"And me," grinned Stretch.

"Before you give us any back-talk, take a look at George and his buddies," advised Larry.

"Well," frowned Floyd, "when you put it that way . . ."

"Let's go," said Larry. He eyed the packroll lashed behind Floyd's saddle and asked, "That all your gear?"

"That's everything," said Floyd, as he swung astride. "I've been travelin' light."

He walked his horse away from the sidewalk and the crowd. The Texans got mounted and followed him along the main stem to the northern outskirts and onward.

"Timbered ridge up ahead—about two miles," Larry observed. "That's where we'll nightcamp."

"How come you jaspers knew my name?" demanded Floyd. "What's the idea of . . . ?"

"Ride, and save your questions," muttered Larry. "We'll tell you the score while we're eatin'."

"I got a right to know who I'm ridin' with," insisted Floyd.

"This beanpole pard of mine is Stretch Emerson," said Larry. "I'm Larry Valentine."

"Well, I'm sure obliged . . ." began Floyd.

"Forget it," shrugged Larry.

"One thing I'll say for him," drawled Stretch. "He's likely as salty as his old man. Thought he was gonna back down when them hotheads started crowdin' him. But he stood his ground."

"You fellers know my old man?" prodded Floyd.

"Later," said Larry.

They made the summit of the ridge a few minutes before sundown; time enough to spot a campsite and gather firewood before full dark. Floyd elected to rustle up a fire, while Stretch broke out the provisions and Larry tended the horses. The meal was austere, but substantial, and Floyd was too hungry to complain.

Over supper, Larry told Floyd of the great

change in his father's fortune, the discovery of gold on Double R land, the establishment of a Double R mine, and Robbie's yearning to see his family reunited.

"He hired us to round up all four of you," drawled Stretch, while Floyd sat quiet, blinking dazedly into the fire. "We're kind of partial to your pa, Floyd. We'd likely have offered to handle the chore anyway, even if he wasn't payin' us."

"Old Robbie is our kind of people," Larry said gruffly. "I just hope I can say the same for you and your brother and sisters."

"We've been scrappin' ever since we were knee-high, me and Mike and the girls," muttered Floyd. "I guess we never got along." He roused from his reverie, took a pull at his coffee and fervently assured them, "But we never hated our folks."

"I should hope," frowned Stretch.

"I pulled out because Pa and Ma were frettin' all the time," declared Floyd. "We were short on grub, and things were gettin' worse every day. I figured—with one less mouth to feed— they could manage better."

"Mike and your sisters had the same idea, seems like," said Larry.

"I don't reckon any of us planned on stayin' away the rest of our lives," said Floyd. "We'd have gone back, soon as we had enough cash to help get the spread workin' again." He shook his head in wonderment. "Gold on Double R land. Think of that. Hey!" A new thought occurred to him. "Who's lookin' out for the old folks? They'll need protection now! Every sharper and thief in the territory'll be houndin' 'em!"

"Mine engineer and a couple hired hands are helpin' out," explained Larry. "As for your old man, he's no fool."

"Well . . ." Floyd nodded grudgingly, "I guess he'll make out—till we're all together again." The idea appealed to him. He grinned broadly. "The Riggs reunited. By golly, that'll be a great day at Double R."

"Runt, which way do we travel manana?" asked Stretch. "We've found one. That's three still on the loose."

"You had word of any of 'em?" Larry eyed the redhead expectantly. "Did Mike stay in touch—or your sisters?"

"We weren't much for letter-writin'," shrugged Floyd. "I wouldn't know where to look for 'em. Except maybe Belle. I heard somethin' a week ago, got talkin' to a shotgun guard at a relay station . . ."

"What'd you hear?" prodded Larry.

"He said, when the stage came through Santa Fé, there was this ruckus in a hash-house. He named the place I think." Floyd searched his memory a moment. "Oh, sure. Durkin's Diner, right on the main street. Customer—a big feller —got thrown out of the diner, darn near got trampled by the stage-team."

"The owner bounced some bum that couldn't pay for his lunch," guessed Stretch.

"Well, no," frowned Floyd. "The shotgun guard got curious. He was eatin' at the same hash-house a little later. Seems the big feller took a shine to the waitress—started pawin' her . . ."

"So the owner threw him out," nodded Stretch.

"Well, no," said Floyd. "It was the waitress threw him out."

"The waitress?" challenged Larry.

"After she'd clobbered him with a chair," said Floyd. "Yeah. And the shotgun guard recalled she was a beautiful redhead, tall and proud and plenty tough. He heard the owner call her Belle. Uh huh. That'd be big sister

Isabelle." He nodded emphatically. "Different from little Nora. Any feller tried foolin' with Nora, she'd scream for help—or swoon maybe. But not Belle. No siree. It was my sister Belle bounced that galoot in Sante Fé. I'd stake my life on it."

"Santa Fé is close," said Stretch.

"North a ways," nodded Floyd. "That's where I was headed—when Soldado Peak got too hot for me." He grimaced in disgust. "Those damn fool women. I tip my hat and, next thing I know, half a dozen hombres are hollerin' for my blood. I swear I didn't try to spark 'em. It's like they were flies and I was a honeypot."

"You got my sympathy, friend," Stretch said very seriously, "on accounta I been havin' the same trouble everyplace I go."

"You're supposed to be asleep," scowled Larry, "before you start dreamin'."

"Jealous," jeered Stretch. "Always jealous."

Larry drained his tin cup and gestured impatiently.

"Throw another hunk of wood on the fire and let's hit the hay."

"Santa Fé's close," offered Floyd. "We could

make it by noon tomorrow, if we get movin' early."

They started out again in the hour before dawn, after a hurried breakfast washed down with black coffee. And, just as Floyd Rigg had predicted, they made bustling, noisy Santa Fé in the heat of noon.

Durkin's Diner was easily located, but the woman waiting on the midday trade was no willowy, boldly-attractive redhead. Blonde, plump and middle-aged, she listened to their question and jerked a thumb to the kitchen.

"You better go ask Durkin."

The proprietor, a balding, sad-eyed little man, had mixed memories of Belle Rigg.

"Best waitress I ever had," he told them, "and the most trouble. Oh, she was honest enough. Good worker too. We got along fine and Lucy—that's my wife—her and Belle were like sisters." He sighed heavily. "But I had to let her go."

"I'm her brother," announced Floyd, "so I guess I got a right to ask why you fired her."

"Nothin' personal against Belle," shrugged Durkin. "She couldn't help bein' beautiful— with a shape that starts the customers droolin'. Scarce a day passed that she din't tangle with some damn fool that couldn't keep his hands to himself, you know? Customers were fightin' over her. Last time, the law didn't get here fast enough and they almost wrecked the place." He shook his head sadly. "So I had to let her go."

"Well . . ." frowned Floyd.

"And maybe she'll be happier now—but I wouldn't bet my life on it," said Durkin. "I just can't imagine Belle wed to John Lucas Junior— livin' in that fancy mansion with old John Senior and Milly and . . ."

"Belle's gettin' married?" gasped Floyd.

"Take it easy," soothed Larry. "Good-lookin' women are scarce. You might've guessed she'd get courted sooner or later."

"But Mister Durkin acts mournful," fretted Floyd, "like he was talkin' about a funeral instead of a weddin'."

"Look, I got chores," said Durkin. He gestured to the stove and the thin woman frying steaks. "You talk to my wife. She'll explain what I mean." He called to her. "Lucy, honey, here's Belle's brother come to ask about her."

Floyd and the Texans joined Lucy Durkin at the stove and began sweating; the heat was intense. The thin woman greeted them affably, and a mite wistfully. Questioned by Floyd, she confided,

"It'd be what they call a marriage of convenience. That poor girl doesn't love young John Lucas—him with his pink face and his buck teeth. But it's the best offer she's had, and she's desperate. We had to let her go. Well, how's she gonna eat? How's she gonna keep herself decent in a town like Santa Fé? She couldn't hold any kind of job . . ."

"Ma'am, my sister ain't afeared of hard work," protested Floyd.

"I know that," Lucy Darkin assured him. "It's not that she wasn't willin' to work hard. It's just—nobody could afford to hire her. Everyplace she shows herself, men start fightin' over her. They broke a window at the Bon Ton when Belle was workin' there. And, when she was helpin' out at Cody's Emporium, Cody had to hold off the hooligans with a shotgun—when he should've been waitin' on his customers." She shook a greasy fork under Floyd's nose and grimly opined, "Only reason she's marryin' John Lucas Junior is she craves a safe place to rest her weary head."

"What about this Lucas bunch?" prodded Larry.

94

She sniffed disdainfully.

"John Senior owns a lot of real estate hereabouts, and that big mansion at the north end of town. Richest man in the territory—and I wouldn't trust him any further than I could throw my husband. He's just like his pink-faced, buck-toothed son, only older. As for Milly Lucas, she already picked a wife for her precious son. Gertrude Hammersmith. They were gonna name the day—until young John caught sight of Belle."

"Let me get this straight," frowned Larry. "The old lady don't want her boy to marry Belle, on account of she was savin' him for . . . ?"

"Gertrude Hammersmith—the parson's daughter," nodded Mrs. Durkin.

"But John Senior, he ain't objectin'?" challenged Larry.

"That old lecher," she sneered. "I wouldn't trust him any further than . . ."

"You already said that," interjected Stretch.

"After the weddin', they're gonna live with the groom's family right there in that fancy mansion," she confided. "And what kind of life will she have? Bad enough bein' wife to a milksop like John Junior—without havin' John

Senior spyin' on her all the time, always tryin' to get close to her, tryin' to touch her . . ."

"Hey now." Stretch stared aghast at Larry and Floyd. Basically a simple soul, the taller Texan was shocked to the core. "Hey now— this ain't right. We can't let her . . ."

"You bet your Texas boots we can't let her," growled Larry.

"There'll be no weddin'," Floyd grimly announced. "The way it sounds to me, sister Belle bit off a mite more'n she can chew. She's in a fix, and I got to get her out of it."

"You mean we're gonna get her out of it," corrected Larry. "Ma'am, where do we find Miss Belle?"

"The Lucas house—the mansion, they call it," said Mrs. Durkin. "The weddin's set for next Saturday, but she had to move in with them a week ago. Wasn't anywhere else she could stay. Poor girl's near broke. Had to sell her clothes to pay for the damage, after she moved out of the Kellard Hotel. Same darn thing. Bunch of lovesick hooligans tried to fight their way into her room—busted a lot of furniture . . ."

"Belle ought never have left the old Double R," opined Floyd.

"They're havin' the engagement party up at the house right now," offered Mrs. Durkin. "All the high-toned folks'll be there. Mayor Carpis and his family, and the Hammersmiths and the . . ."

"Well, doggone it, them Lucas's are about to meet three uninvited guests," declared Floyd. "No sister of mine is gonna hitch up with a man she don't want—just for the sake of a roof over her head. It ain't decent!"

"I told you she's desperate," Mrs. Durkin reminded him. "And you better be careful. John Lucas got a lot of influence hereabouts. He's second cousin to the sheriff. Anything old John wants, he gets. Money talks, he says."

"He ain't gettin' Belle," countered Floyd. "Consarn him, his money don't talk *that* loud."

"Time's a'wastin'," said Larry. "Let's join the party."

The pre-wedding party was the big event of Santa Fé's social season, until the uninvited guests arrived. They rode toward the grassy rise overlooking the northern outskirts of town and were duly impressed by the Lucas mansion, a handsome double-storied structure occupying the summit of the rise, complete with tiled roof and wrought-iron balconies and shaded porch, surrounded by a flower garden and staffed by a small army of servants. Obviously, John Senior believed in doing it in style. The guests were accommodated on a broad stretch of lawn to the left of the house. A gaily-striped canvas marquee had been specially erected for the occasion and, under its shade, the guests moved about tables piled high with food. An outdoors bar had been improvised, and a deputy sheriff stood guard at the archway that marked the southern border of the Lucas estate.

"Nothin' but the best," observed Stretch, as they rode toward the archway. "Everything rich and fancy."

"This Lucas hombre lives high, wide and handsome," Floyd conceded. "But the hell with him. I can't see Belle in this kind of set-up. She'd be out of her class."

"I hear music," frowned Larry. "Damned if they don't have a Mexican band up there— along with all them bartenders in white jackets."

They reached the archway and made to ride through, but were curtly challenged by the deputy, who barred their way and said his piece from behind a leveled shotgun.

"Turn back, boys. This here's a private party."

"You have to let us through," insisted Floyd. "Damnitall, I'm Belle Rigg's brother."

"Oh, sure," leered the deputy. "And my Uncle Julius is president of the whole United States. Who d'you think you're foolin'? Think I don't know a bunch of saddletramps when I see 'em? Turn those horses and get the hell out of here."

"Listen, you don't understand . . ." began Floyd.

"Let me tell him," drawled Larry, as he dismounted.

"Watch it, stranger!" warned the deputy. He was flabby and aggressive, mean-eyed and surly. "I didn't say you could cool your saddle!"

Floyd held his breath, as Larry advanced to within arm's length of the deputy, who made to thumb back a hammer of the shotgun.

"Easy," chided Larry. He grinned into the truculent face, raised a hand and gripped the barrels, then slowly shoved them upward. "You weren't gonna cock this thing, were you? Want to blow me apart? Your boss wouldn't appreciate you killin' a stranger at the front

99

gate. Bad luck. A shootin'—right when all them high-toned folks are havin' a party."

"Let go of the shotgun, mister!" gasped the deputy.

"Why, sure," said Larry. He wrenched the weapon from the lawman's grasp, almost pulling him off his feet. He broke it, ejected the cartridges, then flung it over his shoulder. "Now, let's you and me get somethin' straight, Deputy . . ."

"By Judas, you're askin' for it," breathed the deputy.

He made to empty his holster, but Larry beat him to it. His left hand flashed out and, before the deputy could reach his gun-butt, the pistol was clear of the holster and hurtling over Larry's shoulder.

"Step clear now," ordered Larry. "We're here to see Miss Belle, and we got no time to waste."

The deputy, red-faced, trembling in rage, aimed a kick at Larry's groin—and paid for it. Larry backstepped, caught the upraised boot and twisted. With a wild yell, the deputy spun off-balance. Larry let go of his foot and he pitched into the dust, but scrambled up again, mouthing oaths, brandishing his fists. He swung with his left and missed Larry's head by a full twelve inches, then threw all his muscle behind a driving right. Larry ducked and, as the deputy's fist flashed past his head, unwound an uppercut. The deputy's head jerked back. His back arched and his feet parted company with the ground. Floyd winced to the resounding thud, as he struck ground shoulders-first. This time, he stayed down, well and truly unconscious.

"Tag me," growled Larry, as he remounted. They moved through the gateway and hustled their horses up the walk toward the marquee.

Elegantly gowned, her fire-red tresses fashionably dressed, Isabelle Rigg wrestled with her misgivings and exchanged pleasantries with the guests. She was masking her true feelings behind a serene smile, nodding graciously, sipping punch and wishing it were a double-shot of rye whiskey. Seated between her fiance and her future father-in-law and surrounded by Santa Fé's upper crust, she surveyed them all and asked herself,

"What in blazes are you doing here? How did you get involved with these high-and-mighty ladies and their dude menfolk? And just how happy do you think you'll be, with a husband

101

like John Junior—and a father-in-law like John Senior?"

Her fiance touched her hand and mumbled. She leaned closer to catch his words. John Junior always mumbled. Like father like son. The old man mumbled—softly, suggestively, with his yellowing teeth bared in a knowing leer. It was a dismal prospect, the certainty that, within a decade or so, her husband would become a replica of his sire.

"All the best folks're here, Belle honey," mumbled the son. "Biggest celebration since last Fourth of July."

"All come to see our purty Belle," mumbled the father, gripping her other hand.

She tried to conceal her revulsion. In his early 50s, John Lucas Senior was overweight from self-indulgence, expensively tailored, wealthy, influential and oversexed. After twenty-five years of marriage to the tightly-corsetted Milly —sitting with the Hammersmiths at a nearby table and loudly comforting the weeping Gertrude—the old reprobate still considered himself a ladies' man, a gay blade, God's gift to loney womanhood. The bottom lip drooped and saliva dribbled from a corner of the sagging mouth, as he chuckled raspily and remarked,

"She's gonna be real happy with us, huh son?"

"I aim to do my best," grinned John Junior.

"And your evil old pappy would do his worst, if I gave him half a chance," reflected Belle. She surveyed the gathering again, noting the leading citizens moving past, some pausing to nod respectfully to their host. "That's right. Show respect. Lick his boots—because you owe him money." Her gaze switched to Milly Lucas, who was eyeing her resentfully while murmuring sympathetic remarks to the still-weeping Gertrude. "Some fine celebration—I don't think. The bridegroom too dumb to realize his pa is a chaser—who'll likely chase his bride. The bridegroom's ma hating my insides, wishing her boy was marrying that skinny, flat-chested Gertrude. And I'm supposed to be the guest of honor! Isabelle Jane Rigg, you must be out of your natural mind."

She was turning to frown at the leering John Senior, about to tell him to keep his fat paws to himself, about to announce she had changed her mind and wouldn't marry his pink-faced son if he were the last eligible man on earth, when her gaze fastened on the three horsemen reining up a few yards from the marquee.

The strangers dismounted, ignoring the curious stares of the guests and the challenge muttered by the sheriff. She stared hard at the lean redhead and felt her heart leap.

"Floyd!"

Roughly, she shook her hands free. Lucas Senior and Junior mumbled protests, as she rose and hurried forward to greet her brother.

"Hey, Big Sis!" he yelled, grinning broadly. "It's me!"

Many a time in the past, in the heat of a quarrel, she had hurled herself at her brother, clawing like a wildcat. Now, she flew into his arms, embraced him and planted a kiss on his cheek. Floyd eyed her worriedly, wondering if she would burst into tears. She seemed to be laughing and weeping simultaneously.

"Easy now, Sis," he frowned. "No call to get all wrought up. Everything's gonna be just fine."

"Miss Belle," said Larry. "If you got your heart set on hitchin' up with this Lucas jasper, we won't interfere. But, if it happens you've changed your mind . . ."

"What the hell're you waitin' for?" John Senior ranted at the sheriff. "Get those no-good saddletramps out of here! Who do they think they are—foolin' with my future daughter-in-law?"

"Unhand my fiancee!" mumbled Junior.

"Sis, you don't have to tie up with these Lucas's," Floyd assured her. "I got big news for you. Pa found gold at the old Double R. He owns a gold-mine now—you hear what I'm tellin' you . . . ?"

"Glor-eee hallelujah!" whooped Belle.

"And he wants for all of us to come home," grinned Floyd. "We're gonna find Mike and Nora and head back to the old Double R. So how d'you like that?"

"I'll tell you how I like it!" gasped Belle. "I wasn't going through with this wedding anyway! I was about to break the engagement when you showed up!" She whirled to confront the Lucas men, who were barging out of the marquee with Milly and Gertrude in tow. "You hear that, John Junior? It's all off! I'm setting you free and, believe me, it's a pleasure! Now you can marry Gertrude and make your mother happy! Here's your ring . . ." She tugged it from her finger and tossed it to him. "Thanks for nothing! I'm staying single—till I find me a *real* man!"

"She can't mean it!" raged John Senior. "No

woman in her right mind'd pass up a chance to be my daughter-in-law!"

Belle laughed triumphantly, undismayed by the shocked stares of the guests. The sheriff was blinking uncertainly at the Lucas's and at Belle and her brother—hugging each other with glee. Gertrude Hammersmith wasn't weeping now, but Milly was. And John Senior was livid, sweating in a fever of fury and frustration.

"No woman in her right mind . . . !" he began again.

"I must've been crazy!" Belle retorted. "Thinking I could be happy—living with folks like you!"

"Sheriff, she don't know what she's saying . . ." In his fury, John Senior went to wild extremes. "This is an attempted kidnapping! How do we know this galoot is her brother! Arrest him!"

"Now just a cotton-pickin' minute . . . !" began Stretch.

"Arrest them too," ordered John Senior.

"Try it," Larry sourly invited the lawman, "and I'll make you eat your badge."

While the Lucas men yelled abuse and condemnation at Floyd and the Texans, the deputy added to the confusion by barging onto

106

the scene and loudly complaining he had been assaulted by Larry. Bloody-mouthed and irate, he brandished his shotgun again. Stretch took it for granted the weapon had been reloaded and promptly grabbed for its barrels. The guests began a wild scatter. The sheriff gasped a warning.

"Johnson—don't cock that thing . . . !"

The weapon discharged with a roar and, because Stretch had forced the muzzles upward, there were no casualties. But the charge of buckshot severed one of the poles supporting the marquee, causing the great awning to sag and enshroud a dozen guests, as well as their wildly-cursing host.

Stretch lifted the deputy and hurled him, knocking several more guests to the ground and overturning a couple of chairs. Larry grasped at Floyd's shoulder and growled a command.

"Put your sister on your horse—and let's get out of here!"

"Hold on, you!" yelled the sheriff.

He was rushing Larry, groping for his holstered Colt, when Stretch thrust out a boot and tripped him. As the lawman sprawled, yelling, Stretch made a dash for his pinto. Floyd boosted Belle astride his horse and

107

climbed up after her, and Larry straddled his sorrel. They heeled the animals to a run and made a wild descent to the gateway, leaving confusion in their wake.

There was no conversation for the next quarter-hour. They concentrated on putting plenty of distance between themselves and the Lucas mansion, figuring John Senior might well decide to order a pursuit. But, when they reached the entrance to a pass through the mountains and paused to spell their mounts, a survey of the Santa Fé area revealed all was quiet. No posse surging across the prairie below.

They cooled their saddles. Larry declared the situation called for a stiff shot from the bottle in his saddlebag, and won no argument from his traveling companions. The bottle was brought to light and half-emptied by Floyd and the Texans. And then, noting Belle's wistful expression, Larry broke out a tin cup and handed it to her.

"Say 'when'," he grunted, as he began pouring.

To his surprise, Belle didn't say "when" until the cup was three-quarters full. Then, seating herself on a flat rock, she drank gratefully and stared away toward Santa Fé. Her brother thought to explain.

"It ain't that she's a regular drinkin' woman. It's just, when she needs to calm down, a shot of rye is mighty welcome."

"Pa struck gold," she mused. "Imagine it. After all his years of bad luck, he strikes it rich."

Sitting that way, garbed in her gown of striped silk, her lustrous hair glowing in the sunlight, the Texans considered her one of the most beautiful women they had ever seen. The gown was not designed to withstand the rigors of mountain travel; they would have to replace it as soon as possible. In the meantime, Belle Rigg improved the scenery—and then some.

She finished her share of the whiskey, returned the cup to Larry and remarked to her brother,

"I don't care about leaving my clothes behind. Didn't have much of a wardrobe left anyway."

"It's been rough for you," he guessed.

"Hard to find a place to settle," she frowned. "I guess most women'd be thankful for a good figure. Mine was getting to be more trouble than it's worth. I've had my fill of being pawed at and slobbered over, and that's the pure truth. It's nothing to brag about, believe you me." She raised her eyes to study her brother's face. "And you haven't been doing so good since you quit Double R. Don't try to tell me otherwise, brother. I could always tell when you're lying."

"It's kind of funny at that," he grinned. "I've been havin' the same trouble. I swear I never played fast and loose with any women, but folks keep claimin' I do." Thoughtfully, he opined, "We'd have had to go home anyway, Belle. I mean, even if things were just the same, even if Pa hadn't found gold."

"How desperate could I get?" Belle was still thinking of her narrow escape. "Oh, Lord. I almost got to be Mrs. John Lucas Junior, and that's about the worst thing could happen to any woman." It finally occurred to her to ask, "How'd you find me—and who're your friends?"

The Texans doffed their Stetsons as Floyd performed introductions. He went on to recount the events leading up to the fracas in Soldado Peak, adding,

"Pa hired 'em to round up all four of us, and I was the first."

"We're beholden, Floyd and I." She offered

the drifters an amiable smile. "No offense, but how come Pa hired you?"

"That's somethin' *I'm* curious about," said Floyd. "Now that he's rich, he could've paid to have the Pinkertons hunt us down. Some big detective agency, you know? Pinkertons or Remingtons."

"And that," declared Larry, "is somethin' *I'm* curious about."

"You mean Pa asked a couple strangers to . . ." began Belle.

"By the time your pa got around to hirin's us, we weren't strangers," said Larry.

"Old pals, your pa and us," grinned Stretch. "Cattlemen stick together."

"He said he tried to hire the Pinkertons, but they couldn't spare any men for a search," drawled Larry. "And that don't add up. Big outfit like the Pinkertons. Branch offices all over. Hundreds of special investigators on the payroll." He shook his head emphatically. "I never before heard of the Pinkertons refusin' such a chore."

"But they did," frowned Floyd.

"Your old man ain't much for letter-writin' —that so?" challenged Larry.

"Belle and me and Mike and Nora, we all

had some book-learnin'," said Floyd. "But Pa can scarce read nor write."

"All right, tell me somethin'," frowned Larry. "How well do you know Drake Bonner, the sharper that runs the Rialto Saloon? Is he a special friend of the old man?"

"I never thought so," shrugged Floyd. "Mike used to hang around the Rialto, but Bonner didn't care much about Pa."

"Bonner wrote the letter to the Pinkertons, your pa said," offered Larry.

"That's—uh—kind of strange," opined Floyd.

"Later on, Bonner showed your pa a letter, said it was from the Pinkertons," muttered Larry. "Said they couldn't help him." He fished out his makings and began building a smoke, the while he eyed Belle and her brother pensively. "I never saw that letter from the Pinkertons. Old Robbie tore it up, he said."

"Just what're you getting at?" Belle demanded.

"I ain't real sure what it's all about," Larry confessed. "All I know is I don't trust Bonner . . ."

"He's a sharper—we know that for a fact," interjected Stretch.

"I don't trust Bonner," Larry repeated, "and I don't believe the Pinkerton agency would refuse this kind of job. It's their specialty."

"That's somethin' to think about," said Floyd.

"Something else we'd better think about," said Belle, rising and gesturing impatiently. "Larry and Stretch are getting paid to round up four runaways—and the job's only half-finished."

5

Bounty on a Four-Legged Killer

AT midnight, Herb Mathews rode into the sheltered cleft in a rock-wall high in the mountains, the clatter of his mount's hooves rousing the five men by the fire. They rolled over and watched, as he swung down and began offsaddling. Shemp sat up with his blanket draped about his shoulders and asked,

"How far ahead?"

"Too far off to see our smoke," said Mathews. He tethered his horse with the other animals and trudged across to join his cronies, toting his blanket-roll. "And I made sure they didn't spot me. Spied on 'em through the telescope. They're camped in the northern foothills."

"Same bunch?" prodded Shemp.

"For sure," nodded Mathews. "Except there's four of 'em now. They got a woman with 'em—red-haired like the hombre they collected in Soldado Peak."

114

"And he ain't the one we're after?"

"He ain't the one. He's no sawed-off. Lean jasper—taller than the one we're after."

"Well, long as you know where they're camped," shrugged Shemp, "cuttin' their sign tomorrow is gonna be an easy chore."

"Quite a chase they're leadin' us," Mathews remarked, as he rolled into his blankets. "But I ain't complainin'. I'd tag 'em from here to Canada for that extra fifteen hundred."

"Easy money," muttered Shemp. "One bullet is all it takes. And then we collect." He reached for a chunk of wood, tossed it onto the fire, stared across at Mathews and asked, "Why d'you suppose Bonner wants him dead? Twenty-five hundred—that's a helluva price to pay for one man's life."

"I don't care a damn about Bonner's reasons," retorted Mathews, as he closed his eyes. "All I care about is his money."

All was quiet at the camp in the foothills. Belle Rigg slept soundly, wrapped in Larry's poncho and Stretch's spare blanket. Her brother slumbered close by, snoring steadily. Maybe the Riggs were uncommonly weary; neither heard the distant, ominous sound that roused the Texans.

115

Larry threw his blanket aside and sat up, his hand on his holstered Colt. A few feet away, his partner nudged his hat off his face and traded stares with him. They waited, listening intently, and then the sound was repeated, a guttural growl carried clear on the night air. Larry held a finger to his lips, signaling Stretch to silence. The taller Texan nodded. They got to their feet and, with their blankets draped about their shoulders, moved away from the fire. Not until they were out of earshot did they pause to trade comments, keeping their voices low.

"That's no bobcat, as if you haven't guessed," grunted Stretch.

"Mountain lion," opined Larry. "And he's no cub. Got his full growth, nothin' surer."

"A big one—and ornery," muttered Stretch. "Well? You got any other ideas?"

"He knows we're here," frowned Larry. "Caught our scent by now. Might come snoopin' by and by."

"Smelled our supper," guessed Stretch. "The chow was better this time, on account of Belle's good cookin'."

"Not many cougars'll come lookin' for trouble," mused Larry. "Most times, they're leery of humans. But this big cat might get curious enough . . ."

"Or hungry enough," said Stretch. "Or just plain mean."

"Go back to sleep," ordered Larry. "I'll sit guard. When I can't stay awake any more, I'll rouse you and you can take over."

After Stretch had settled down again, Larry armed himself with his Winchester and made a patrol of some 40 yards of the area surrounding the camp. The horses nickered uneasily when the marauding cougar growled again, this time farther away, but still audible. Until 3.30, Larry hunkered beyond the firelight, nursing his rifle, listening intently and probing the gloom through narrowed eyes.

Six yawns in a row warned him it was time to rouse his partner. The taller Texan sat guard until daybreak, then built up the fire, broke out provisions and roused Larry and the Riggs.

Belle immediately announced her intention of bathing.

"We forded a stream a little ways back," she reminded them. "Won't take me but a few minutes to get washed up, and then I'll be back to fix breakfast."

117

"Yeah, okay," frowned Larry. "But you better have some company."

"*That'll* be the day," she countered.

"I mean brother Floyd," he patiently explained, nodding to her kinsman. "And listen, amigo, take your rifle along."

"What . . . ?" began Floyd.

"No call to fret," soothed Stretch. "It's just we heard a big cat prowlin' round. No sense takin' chances."

Within the half-hour, the men had shaved, Belle had completed her ablutions and prepared a substantial breakfast, which they attacked with gusto. And, during that meal, the marauder snarled a challenge that started the horses stamping and snorting. Larry shrugged resignedly.

"Nothin' else we can do but go find him," he opined.

"Well, if you have to . . ." began Belle.

"He ain't about to quit, this critter," warned Larry. "If we broke camp rightaway, he'd likely tag us. Maybe he made a kill in the last couple days—and he still craves the taste of blood."

"So it's him—or maybe one of us," said Floyd.

"It could end up that way," nodded Larry.

"You wait here. And stick close to big sister, understand?"

"We go afoot?" asked Stretch.

"Reckon so," said Larry, as he unbuckled his spurs. "He'd hear horses easier than he'd hear us."

The Texans moved northwest from the campsite, descending toward a stand of timber with their rifles at the ready. Shielded—or so they thought—by a line of boulders, they heard the big cat again, this time a full-throated roar, echoing, challenging.

Stretch grimaced and muttered,

"I could swear he's seen us—and he's sayin' 'Keep a'comin', boys, I'm waitin' for you.' Kinda spooky, huh?"

"If he jumps you and claws you dead, I'll let daylight through him," Larry promised.

"Thanks a heap," scowled Stretch. "That makes me feel better about the whole thing."

They made the timberline and advanced into the shade of the trees, moving slowly along a natural corridor roofed by low-hanging branches. Larry pantomimed his strategy, patting his rifle's barrel and nodding straight ahead, then gesturing upward. Stretch got the message. They continued their slow advance

119

and, while Larry watched the area in front of them and scanned the timber to either side, Stretch kept his gaze turned upward, watching the branches.

When they had almost reached the north edge of the timber, the big cat challenged them again. Larry heard his partner's mumbled oath and whirled in time to see him cut loose, his Winchester raised high. Only one shot the taller Texan triggered and, abruptly, the cougar's threatening roar ceased. They heard a slithering, rustling sound in the foliage high above. Larry sidestepped instinctively, and the mighty killer thudded to the ground almost at his feet.

Stretch loosed another oath and drew a sleeve across his face.

"You were right, I reckon," he muttered. "He'd never have quit. He was gonna stay after us till he tasted blood again."

"Dead shot," frowned Larry.

"By golly—he's a big one," breathed Stretch.

Sprawled full length, the cougar was an awesome sight, even in death. The width of chest and shoulders, the size of the paws, exceeded the average for an animal of this species; the head was bigger, the neck thicker.

"Dry blood on his paws—and plenty of it," Larry observed.

About to offer another comment, he cocked an ear to the sound of voices. Stretch said,

"That ain't Floyd nor Belle."

"They sound excited," frowned Larry. "Three or four of 'em."

"More like a half-dozen," said Stretch.

The taller Texan's estimate was correct. A few moments later, the men converged on them from three directions, six shabbily-garbed, eager-eyed jaspers, obviously farmworkers, toting rifles and shotguns. They gathered about Larry and Stretch and stared hard and long at the dead cougar, then began cheering. Two of them actually danced with glee. Another raised his eyes to the sky and fervently declared,

"He done heeded our prayers, durned if He didn't!"

A scrawny, bearded man, obviously the group's leader, confronted the Texans, offered his name, his hand and an explanation. It transpired Jethro Pinchley and his friends were the elders of a farming community located in a basin a short distance from the foothills. For a month or more, their stock had been slaugh-

121

tered and their people constantly menaced by the lone killer.

"Seemed like he'd be hauntin' us forever," Pinchley declared. "We come a'huntin' him time and time again, but he was like a ghost. Couple of us glimpsed him once or twice, tried to draw a bead on him. He was always too fast for us."

"I swear we were gettin' used to him," a younger man remarked.

"That's my son Warren," offered Pinchley.

"We even gave him a name," Warren told the Texans. "We called him Bloody Bill."

"Named him after Bill Bascombe," explained Pinchley. "This Bascombe was a land agent and a money-lender back in Hattonsburg, Kansas. Mighty mean jasper." He grimaced in contempt. "Wouldn't surprise me if him and the cougar was related."

"We sure are beholden," Warren assured them. "Pa, how's about the bounty?"

"Only fittin', Jethro," asserted another man. "They got Bloody Bill, so . . ."

"My partner downed him," said Larry. "His name's Emerson. Mine's Valentine."

"Pleased to meet you gents," beamed

Pinchley. "And it'll be my pleasure to pay Mister Emerson the bounty."

"We passed the hat a couple weeks back," said Warren. "Collected a whole fifty dollars and agreed we'd pay it to the man that killed Bloody Bill."

"Where you camped?" demanded Pinchley.

"Back a ways," said Larry. "We're travelin' with a lady, Miss Belle Rigg, and her brother Floyd."

"Well, by golly, you go fetch 'em and bring 'em to the basin," invited Pinchley. "I've been savin' a jug to celebrate our deliverance from Bloody Bill. You and your friends gonna be our guests, hear? No arguments. Go fetch 'em, while me and the boys take this cat home. Might's well use his hide."

The Texans and the farmers parted temporarily. Back at their camp, Larry explained the situation to the Riggs, and Stretch flatly declared,

"I don't feel like takin' no fifty dollar bounty from these folks. I looked 'em over real careful, Jethro and his pards, and I'm bettin' they're dirt-poor. To a bunch like them, fifty dollars is durn near a fortune."

"I noticed too," nodded Larry.

123

"But, if they're offerin' hospitality . . ." began Floyd.

"It wouldn't be polite to refuse," opined Belle.

"We'll help 'em celebrate," suggested Larry. "And maybe Stretch'll figure how to refuse their fifty dollars—without insultin' anybody."

"You tell 'em for me, runt," begged Stretch. "When it comes to sweet-talkin', you're smarter'n me."

They descended the south slopes of the basin some 30 minutes later and made for the farm dead centre of its verdant floor. The other farms were scattered about the slopes and rim of the big hollow and, from them, men, women and children were moving down to the Pinchley homestead. Floyd, surveying the plowed fields and the neat oblongs of green, remarked,

"It took these folks quite a time to raise a pay-crop. Guess they'll do all right from now on."

"But, up till now, they've had it rough," guessed Larry. "And Bloody Bill made it rougher for 'em—cuttin' out their milk cows and a plow-horse or two."

Stretch was accorded a hero's welcome by the people of the basin. Small boys jostled one another for the privilege of being allowed to touch the Winchester that had toppled the tawny killer. There were handshakes all round, and Jethro Pinchley, urged on by his neighbors, clambered onto a box on his front porch and made a speech. The jug—and several others just like it—came to light and were passed from hand to hand.

As diplomatically as possible, Larry explained his partner's reluctance to accept the $50 bounty.

"It ain't as if we set out to earn a bounty," he told the people. "Only reason we hunted Bloody Bill was we figured he was huntin's us. Had to be him or us, you understand? And, besides, my partner's superstitious. It runs in his family. The Emersons of Texas claim it's bad luck to take money for killin' a cougar before noon or a wolf after sundown—or a rattlesnake on Sunday."

Pinchley and his neighbors were finally persuaded to keep the $50, but were adamant in their determination to do something for the travelers, to make some small gesture of appreciation. Belle then complicated the issue by offering to trade her fine silk gown for some utilitarian garb. There could be no guessing how long it would take them to locate Nora and Mike, or how far they would have to search, and her party gown was somewhat less than adequate for a long journey on horseback. Pinchley's elder daughter was of similar physique. She studied Belle's gown in rapt admiration and offered her Sunday gingham, but insisted this was small payment for such a treasure. Would Belle also accept her bonnet and shawl, also the bottle of cologne bequeathed her by her Aunt Beulah, plus a framed portrait of General Grant?

"All I need is that gingham gown," smiled Belle, taking her arm.

While Belle was changing in Rose Pinchley's bedroom, her brother won Larry and Floyd's interest with a chance remark. He had never seen a redhaired woman as beautiful as Belle, except on one other occasion, and just a week ago at that.

"Same color," he declared. "Yup. Just as red as yours and Miss Belle's. Actress-lady she was. Some shorter'n Miss Belle, but just as purty."

"By golly . . ." began Floyd.

"Let him tell it all," drawled Larry. "Might be our luck's about to change again."

"I said somethin' wrong?" frowned Warren.

126

"More likely you said somethin' *right*," countered Larry. "Keep talkin', boy. Tell us where you saw this other redhead."

"It was in Stubbsville a week back," said Warren. "Mule-freighter paid me fifteen dollars to help him deliver a heavy load. Sewin' machines for a storekeeper, you know? The freighter's regular partner had a busted arm . . ."

"About the redhead," prodded Floyd.

"Well, after we delivered the shipment and Mister Bailey paid me off, I stopped by this hall where these play-actor folks were puttin' on a show." The farmer's son paused to heave a sigh. "Twenty-five cents a ticket. A whole quarter. My gosh. But it was worth it, just to see that little fire-haired lady—her so beautiful —and so sad . . ."

"Her name?" frowned Larry.

"It sounded Irish . . ."

"Irish?"

"What I mean—it started with O. Most folks are Irish, if their name starts with O. Ain't that so?"

Larry and Floyd traded glances.

"She might've changed her name," Floyd opined.

"Is Nora the kind of girl who'd join up with a bunch of play-actors?" asked Larry.

"Hell!" snorted Floyd. "You could bet your life on it. Ever since she was a little sprig she's been makin' believe—always pretendin'. Dressin' up in Ma's clothes, tryin' to talk like a high-toned lady."

"It was real sad, that play," recalled Warren. "I didn't understand hardly any of it. They was talkin' English—but I never heard talkin' like that before. I guess it was poetical. And the boss-actor—I swear he was gallivantin' around in tights."

"Tights?" blinked Floyd.

"Black tights," Warren nodded grimly. "Well, I guess them actor fellers got no shame, no shame at all." On an afterthought, he added, "I fetched the playbill home."

"You mean-uh-with all their names—the parts they played and such?" prodded Floyd.

"We'd admire to take a look at that playbill, Warren," said Larry.

"Listen, we're all beholden to you gents," said Warren, "and you can have anything I own —but . . ."

"Fetch the playbill," urged Larry.

"I ain't never gonna let it go," declared

128

Warren. "It's all I got to remember her by—that purty little redhead . . ."

"We don't want to keep it," Larry patiently assured him. "We only want to look at it."

Warren hurried into the house. Rejoining them a few moments later, he held the folded paper tenderly, as if it were something of great value. Larry took it from him, unfolded it and, with Floyd peeking over his shoulder, observed,

"They call 'emselves the Montrose Repertory."

"And the play was called Hamlet," said Floyd. "By William—what kind of a name is that?"

"Shakespeare," said Larry. "I've seen it before. A playwriter. English I think."

They studied with keen interest the list of characters.

"Ophelia," frowned Larry.

"Told you it started with an O," offered Warren.

"Ophelia," Larry repeated. "And alongside of that—the name of the girl who . . ."

"Noretta Rigg La Rue." Floyd snorted again. "The nerve of that sassy little . . ."

"Mind how you talk about her," chided Warren.

"'Scuse me all to pieces," grinned Floyd, returning the precious playbill.

"Stubbsville—how far?" demanded Larry.

"North—up by the Colorado border," Warren told him. "You push straight east from the basin for three miles and you'll reach the crossroads and a signpost. Then you just stay on the north trail, ride it all the way to Stubbsville. No other towns in between. Leastways not on that route."

"Too much to hope they'd still be there," Larry warned Floyd. "These travelin' shows don't stay long in any one place. But we'll make for Stubbsville, find out which way they headed from there."

No sooner had Belle emerged from the house, garbed in checked gingham, than her brother was boosting her onto his sorrel. The Texans bade the farm folk a hasty farewell, got mounted and made for the east slope of the basin with the double-laden Rigg horse following close.

Out of the basin and headed for the crossroads, Floyd answered his sister's questions. When he told her of the playbill and the red-haired actress portraying Ophelia, Belle nodded emphatically and agreed,

"That just has to be little sister."

"Callin' herself Noretta Rigg La Rue," grinned Floyd. "So how d'you like that?"

"When I catch up with the day-dreaming little fool . . ." Belle shrugged resignedly. "I guess I won't know whether I should hug her and kiss her—or turn her over my knee."

Larry set a stiff pace all the way to the shabby border town. They stayed in Stubbsville only long enough to ascertain that the Montrose Repertory had moved on some twelve days before, westbound, and using their own transportation, the company and costumes, provisions and other equipment jam-packed into a couple of covered wagons, a four-seater rockaway and Mr. Chester Montrose's surrey. Before taking to the west trail, they used some of the cash advanced them by Robbie to purchase supplies and extra clothing for Belle.

In the next three days, they passed through four small towns on the route to the San Juan Mountains of Southeastern Colorado, always one jump behind the traveling players. In the fourth settlement, San Mateo, they were told the Montrose outfit had played a one-night stand there and moved on that very morning.

It was sundown and the searchers were

travel-weary, but determined to push on. They planned their next move in a cafe on the edge of town. Larry had gathered useful information from his favorite source—three local bartenders, two stablehands and the barber. Over supper he told his companions,

"Gillsburg is the next town west, just this side of the foothills, and that's where they're bound. This Montrose jasper ain't exactly temperance. He bragged he'd have a big success in Gillsburg—to three different bartenders."

"How far?" demanded Floyd.

"And how long will it take, with two of us riding double?" asked Belle.

"The stablehand figures we could make it by sundown tomorrow," said Larry.

"If . . . ?" prodded Stretch.

"As if you haven't guessed," shrugged Larry. "We'd have to leave right after supper, travel that west trail till midnight, make camp and push on at sun-up."

"Oh, my achin' callouses," sighed Stretch.

"Too rough for you, Belle?" asked Larry.

"Our horses'll be rested by the time we finish supper," Belle said briskly.

"And I don't reckon we'd enjoy stayin' overnight in San Mateo," shrugged Floyd.

"So . . ." said Larry.

"We push on," nodded Belle.

"That's what I was afeared you'd say," growled Stretch.

The trail wound through sagebrush and yucca like a serpent in torment, with the peaks and crags of the San Juans clearly visible in the moonlight. Moving a quarter-mile ahead of Stretch and the Riggs, Larry eagerly scanned the foothills. But it was too early to hope for a glimpse of the lights of Gillsburg.

At midnight, they walked their weary mounts off the trail, moving toward the sound of running water until the rippling stream came into view. Larry called a halt on a strip of grass by the south bank. He listened to the night-sounds, while Stretch looked to the comfort of the animals. Belle flopped onto a blanket, exhausted. She was lying on her side, lapsing into slumber, by the time her brother fetched wood and got a fire going.

"Hearin' mountain cats again?" Floyd asked softly.

"Just a coyote," replied Larry. "And that suits me fine."

"You crave the quiet life, huh?" grinned Floyd.

"Always have," nodded Larry. "Stretch and me both."

"You didn't act so peaceable," chuckled Floyd, "when you tangled with them hotheads in Soldado Peak."

"We play rough when we have to," shrugged Stretch. He stifled a yawn and trudged to the fire, toting his and Larry's packrolls. "Hell, I'm beat."

"Settle down, amigos," muttered Larry. "Got to make a few miles tomorrow."

"We won't make the miles real fast," countered Floyd. "That sorrel of mine works hard, but, with Belle and me ridin' double . . . ."

"Yeah, I know," frowned Larry. "I've been thinkin', if we find your other sister in Gillsburg, we're gonna have to buy a couple extra horses."

"Or put Belle and Nora on the southbound stage," suggested Floyd.

They were talking quietly, assuming Belle was fast asleep. She proved them wrong. Without opening her eyes, she mumbled,

"We won't split up. After we find Nora, we go looking for Mike. When the Riggs go home —they go together."

"Whatever you say, Sis," nodded Floyd.

At sun-up they breakfasted on beans and bacon, a meagre meal quickly disposed of. Belle's excitement was contagious. Some sixth sense told her they would find Nora within the next 48 hours, and Larry wasn't about to argue against feminine intuition.

Their pace slowed in the hour before noon; they had passed through the foothills and were making the climb toward the steeper slopes. For the sake of the double-loaded sorrel, Larry insisted on frequent pauses and, for a mile or more of that tiring ascent, the men walked.

When they sighted the distant lights of the township in the late afternoon, Mathews and his men were less than five miles behind them, deliberately hanging back.

"All of a sudden, I'm not tired any more," murmured Belle.

"She's there," asserted Floyd. "I feel it."

"Everybody's a hunch-player," grinned Stretch.

The familiar playbills were everywhere. They recognized them, as they idled the horses along Gillsburg's main stem, trading friendly nods with the locals. From porch-posts and plank walls, outside barber shops, saloons and livery stables, the posters lured the culture-conscious of the frontier, proclaiming Chester Montrose as the "most celebrated Hamlet since Sir Henry Irving". The searchers surrendered their mounts to the care of a stablehand and eagerly made a closer inspection of a playbill, noting that the role of Ophelia was still being played by Noretta Rigg La Rue.

"You folks rid a long way to see the show, huh?" asked the stablehand.

"Quite a trace," nodded Larry. "And where do we find it—this theatre place?"

"The New Occidental Opera House they call it," offered the stablehand. "Uptown a ways. Corner of Main and Gill. But you'll have to hustle." He checked his watch. "The show starts in twenty minutes."

A few minutes later, Larry and Stretch were striding through the rear entrance of the New Occidental with Belle and Floyd in tow, ignoring the protests of the stage manager,

"No admittance back stage," he chided. "Mister Montrose gave strict orders."

He trotted after them, still mumbling protests, as they entered the passage leading to the dressing rooms. They were drawing abreast of the first room, when the door was opened to reveal a woman in a bright yellow robe. She was a brunette, passably attractive and keeping a firm grip on a china mug. As she drawled a greeting, she swayed slightly. Giggling coquettishly, she lifted the mug and took a swig. Larry added the contents of the mug to her bloodshot eyes, and the answer was not coffee.

"That ain't . . ." began Stretch.

"Of course not," frowned Belle. "You think I wouldn't recognize my own sister?"

"Who're you lookin' for, honey?" asked the brunette, fluttering her lashes at Larry.

"Ma'am, we're here to collect our sister," announced Floyd. "Could be you and her are acquainted? Miss Nora Rigg?"

"You folks kin to little Nora?" The woman showed quick interest. Her eyes were gleaming now, albeit still bloodshot. "And you've come to take her away?"

"We wouldn't take it kindly if anybody tried to stop us," Larry said grimly.

"Stop you? I sure won't stop you!" She chuckled elatedly. "Listen, until that little chick joined up with us, I always played Ophelia. Now, old Chet calls me an understudy." She lifted the mug again. "And I get bored. So I need a little cheer to boost my ego."

"Where do we find her?" demanded Belle.

"Second door along," offered the brunette. "C'mon, I'll show you." She thought to add, as she led them along the passage, "I'm Carlotta Duprez. That's my stage name. My real handle isn't quite so fancy." She pounded on the door and called to the occupant. "Company, dearie!"

"Nora, you come out of there!" cried Belle. "Come out this instant, or I'll tan your hide!"

They heard a gasp from inside the room. The door swung open and Nora dashed out with her pretty face aglow with joy, her eyes ashine. And, again, the drifters marveled that a homely old jasper like Robbie Rigg could sire such beautiful children. Not that Nora was as beautiful as her tall and compelling sister. Hers was a different kind of charm. She was small with a neat figure, her face a pale oval under the characteristic Rigg tresses. Like Carlotta, she wore a robe, deep green and with a sash tightly knotted, emphasizing her trim waist.

"I was never so glad to see anybody," she declared. "What're we gonna fight about?"

"No scrapping this time, little Sis," grinned Floyd, planting a brotherly kiss on her brow. "We got great news. Pa found gold on Double R range. He hired these gents to come find us and fetch us home. No more hard times, kid. The Riggs are in the minin' business now."

"Oh, my!" breathed Nora. "It sounds—too wonderful to be true!" She hugged Belle, flashed the Texans a radiant smile and turned to the brunette. "Isn't that just marvellous, Carlotta? I can leave rightaway, quit the company!"

"Ginger-peachy," smiled Carlotta.

"It means I won't have to play Ophelia tonight," enthused Nora. "Or ever again! You can go on in my place! Mister Montrose won't mind. You're a better actress than me anyway." Very seriously, she informed her brother and sister, "I'm through with the theatre—finished for good and all. I was that scared—every time I went on stage. The way those cowhands and roughnecks whooped and whistled—I declare it was terrifying!"

"What is the meaning of this unseemly disturbance?" Another door had opened, and there now emerged the most startling apparition ever to faze Stretch, who flinched and took a step backward. At close quarters, the somewhat elderly Chester Montrose was a sight to behold with the dilated eyes and sagging jaw. Stretch's eyes dilated. His jaw sagged. "Fennister!" The actor bellowed to the stage-manager. "Remove these vagabonds! Eject them, I command you!"

Larry grinned wryly. Garbed in black from neck to feet, his spindly legs accentuated by his tights, his blond wig slightly awry, the great actor was more ludicrous than impressive. And it was obvious Floyd shared that opinion; he was laughing unrestrainedly, slapping his knee.

"If you please, Mister Montrose, they're too much for me to handle," mumbled the stage-manager.

"Then get thee hence!" boomed Montrose. "Summon the constabulary."

"Mister, you'd better get used to the idea," frowned Belle. "Nora's our sister, and we're taking her out of here. She's through with play-actin'."

"You better believe it, Chet," chuckled Carlotta. "Her old man struck gold, and she's never gonna have to work again. So don't try talkin' her out of it. We're no competition for a goldmine."

"Curse the luck," grunted Montrose. Stretch flinched again, as he removed his wig and scratched his bald dome. "I should've signed the wench to a contract."

Nora had retreated into her dressing room

when the actor appeared. Now, she emerged again, garbed in cotton blouse and black bombazine skirt and donning a straw hat. She passed a bulging carpetbag to her brother, waved cheerfully to Carlotta, then frowned apologetically at her disgruntled ex-boss. To soften the blow, she offered a line from the play.

"Could beauty, my lord, have better commerce than with honesty?"

"Get thee to a nunnery," scowled Montrose.

"She ain't headed for no nunnery," countered Floyd. "We're takin' her home to the old Double R spread in San Jose."

"Curse the luck," muttered Montrose. "Ah! The slings and arrows of outrageous fortune." He gestured resignedly. "To a nunnery go, and quickly too. Farewell."

"I'll be changed and ready for my entrance— right on cue," promised Carlotta, turning away.

"And sober, I hope," sighed Montrose. "If there's one thing I can't abide, it's a tangle-footed Ophelia."

"Come on, kids," smiled Belle. "Let's get out of here."

6

The Thousand Dollar Gunhand

FROM the New Occidental, the Rigg sisters and their escorts proceeded to a hotel in the heart of town. Larry had decreed they should enjoy a few creature comforts before beginning their search for the fourth missing Rigg: the last 48 hours had been arduous.

In the lobby of the Ravenstock Hotel, they consulted with the night-clerk and settled for two doubles and a single on the first floor. The clerk arranged for the porter to take the girl's baggage upstairs, after which Floyd gestured to the dining room entrance and asked,

"What're we waitin' for? It's suppertime. We're all hungry—and Pa gave Larry cash for expenses."

"So we plan our search for brother Mike over a chicken dinner—any arguments?" smiled Belle.

"And I have so much to tell you," declared

142

Nora, "about my career as an actress." Somewhat smugly, she assured her sister, "It was short, but eventful."

They were moving toward the dining room, when Nora heard her name called. She paused to frown at the well-groomed dandy strolling into the lobby, a handsome individual in flashy town clothes. His smile was arrogant and assured. White teeth gleamed under his flowing mustache, as he doffed his beaver hat and accorded her a sweeping bow; he seemed not to have noticed Nora's companions.

"Miss Noretta Rigg La Rue? Permit me to introduce myself. Wade Blain—your servant, ma'am. I saw you arrive at the New Occidental, and looked forward to seeing your performance."

"I will not be performing, Mister Blain," Nora said gently. "Tonight, the part of Ophelia will be played by an actress of far greater talent. So, if you're partial to Shakespeare, I suggest you hurry to the theatre and . . ."

"I made myself a promise, Miss La Rue," declared Blain.

"The name is Rigg," said Nora. "I don't need a stage-name any more, for I have resigned from the profession."

143

"The theatre's loss is Double R's gain," smiled Belle.

"I promised myself the pleasure of your company," grinned Blain. "Supper after the play was what I had in mind but, since you're no longer involved with the theatre, we needn't wait. I made a reservation at the Golden Slipper Restaurant."

The Texans traded frowns. Floyd blinked at Belle and remarked,

"Mighty sure of himself, this hombre."

Calmly ignoring the curious stares of Nora's companions, the dude extended a well-manicured hand.

"You accept my invitation, of course," he drawled.

"On the contrary, sir, I decline," said Nora.

"I insist," Blain said firmly.

"And I," retorted Nora, "intend dining with my sister and brother and our friends."

Suddenly, Blain wasn't smiling. He grimaced in irritation and made to take her arm, asserting,

"Any tent-show woman would jump at the chance."

"Aw, the heck with this," growled Floyd. "Listen, mister . . ."

"Back off," snapped Blain. "This doesn't concern you."

"Well, by golly . . ." began Floyd.

"Easy, feller," chided Stretch. He side-stepped to place himself between Floyd and Blain, then prodded the dude's chest with a hard forefinger. "Now heed this, Fancy Pants. The little lady ain't interested in your invite so, if you're a gentleman, you'll turn right round and hustle out of here. Heard what she said, didn't you?" He prodded harder. "Miss Nora's eatin' with us."

"Keep your hands to yourself, saddletramp!" gasped Blain.

"That does it," sighed Stretch. "'Scuse us, ladies."

The clerk blinked nervously and Blain loosed a startled protest, as Stretch lifted him bodily and toted him to the street entrance. One mighty heave sent him hurtling out to the sidewalk. Nora winced at the sound of Blain's fall, a dull thud followed by a curse of rage. Stretch loafed back to them, grinning unconcernedly, and then Blain reappeared in the entrance. He was disheveled, florid with fury. He had swept his coat-tails back to reveal the gunbelt girding

145

his loins, the pearl butt of the .45 holstered at his right thigh.

"You laid hands on me—damn you!" he accused. "I demand satisfaction!"

"Go chase yourself," invited Stretch.

"Enjoy your supper—but don't try to sleep!" breathed Blain. "You'll have too much to worry about!"

"Is that a fact?" frowned Stretch.

"I'll be waiting for you in the street," announced Blain. "At sunrise, do you hear? You'll come out and face me then, saddletramp, or I'll come looking for you!"

"Now listen, dude . . ." began Stretch.

"The name is Wade Blain," said Blain, with heavy emphasis. "Remember it. And remember our appointment." As he began withdrawing from the doorway, he grinned coldly and added, "Enjoy your supper. It will be your last."

For a few moments after he had departed, the Texans and the Riggs stood quiet, frowning at the entrance. The clerk mopped at his brow with a kerchief and mumbled,

"This is terrible. *Terrible!*"

"Don't sweat," soothed Larry. "Sweatin'll melt your collar and rust your studs."

146

"A gun duel—in the Ravenstock Hotel," gasped the clerk.

"Ain't gonna be no gunfight in here," Stretch assured him. "You heard what the dude said. He wants I should meet him in the street at sun-up." Shrugging nonchalantly, he opined, "By then, he'll be more interested in breakfast than a shootout."

"Don't count on it," retorted Floyd. "That jasper got a mean eye." He frowned reproachfully at Larry, who appeared supremely unconcerned. "Heck, Larry, don't you care what happens to your buddy?"

"What's to worry about?" challenged Larry. "Damn fool likely won't draw on Stretch anyway. And, if he does, he'll wish he hadn't." He took Belle's arm and started for the dining room. "Come on. Let's eat."

Over supper, the Texans refused to discuss the arrogant and aggressive dude. They were more concerned that Floyd and his sisters should compare notes and swap theories as to the whereabouts of their brother, the elusive Mike.

They worked their way through broiled chicken, the specialty of the house, moved on to the dessert and traded hunches. It seemed

147

none of them had any definite word. Nora had heard of a red-haired faro-player in Albuquerque running foul of the local law, but Floyd pointed out,

"That couldn't be our Mike. Faro ain't his game. He don't savvy faro, so he stays away from it. He's a poker-man is Mike."

"In Santa Fé, I heard the deputy talking about a redhead getting lynched in Rambeau Flats. That's somewhere in Utah." This information was offered by Belle, who nodded reassuringly at her brother and sister and told them, "I was fearing the worst, thinking that horse-thief might be brother Mike, till the deputy said he'd also knifed a stablehand."

"Couldn't be Mike," said Floyd.

"You sure?" demanded Larry.

"He might get desperate enough to steal a horse," shrugged Floyd, "but he'd never use a knife. Knives are unlucky for Mike."

"Oh my, yes," agreed Nora. "Pa never let him whittle when he was little."

"With a blade, he's clumsy," explained Floyd. "I swear he couldn't sharpen a pencil without cuttin' three fingers. Besides, Mike's no killer."

"So, when you get right down to it, you got

no notion where we'll find him," said Larry. "And that means we'll have to start with the letter he wrote your pa."

"Where was he then?" asked Floyd.

Larry produced the letters supplied by old Robbie and checked Mike's.

"Written and mailed in Fort Resolution, Arizona Territory."

"I know that town," offered Floyd. "Never been there, but know where it's at. North Arizona. I've seen it on a map. Little ways south of the Carrizo Mountains."

"That makes it southwest of here," frowned Larry. "All right. We rest easy tonight and start for Arizona after breakfast. That gives you plenty time to catch up on your sleep." He nodded to Floyd, then to the sisters. "And you girls'll have plenty to talk about. But don't talk all night, understand?"

"You traveled all the way from Santa Fé with these gentlemen?" Nora eyed her sister uncertainly. "I declare, Belle honey . . ."

"What matters is they *are* gentlemen," chuckled Belle. "And, besides, I had brother Floyd for a bodyguard."

"What's more," said Floyd, "they're workin' for Pa. He hired Larry and Stretch to find us."

149

"Pa was always a good judge of character, so I'll put my trust in these gentlemen." She aimed a shy smile at Larry. "And I thank you, sir, for your hospitality—this elegant supper . . ."

"Thank your pa," shrugged Larry. "It's his money."

Some little time after the travelers had retired to their rooms, the pudgy, slow-moving Deputy Cliff Sandler loafed into the lobby to trade gossip with the night-clerk and was promptly warned of impending disaster.

"There'll be a killing on Main Street at dawn, unless you can stop 'em. Better go tell your boss, Cliff."

The clerk offered a highly-colored account of Stretch's set-to with the trigger-tempered dude, while Sandler fidgeted uneasily.

"You sure about that name?" he asked.

"Sure I'm sure," frowned the clerk. "Called himself Wade Blain. Hey—haven't I heard that name before? Sounds kind of familiar."

"Yeah, well, I better go talk to the sheriff," said Sandler.

The deputy located his boss in a pool parlor at the west end of town. Sheriff Pat Hansbury, as portly, as slow-moving as his deputy, didn't much appreciate being interrupted at his favorite pastime, but put up his cue and followed Sandler out to the street. Under a lamp, they lit cigars and parleyed.

"Blain, huh?" grunted Hansbury. "Well, I knew he was here, but I was hopin' he'd move on."

"Hell, Pat, he's wanted," muttered Sandler. "That killin' at Wilkesville. Thousand dollar reward—dead or alive."

"You thinkin' we should risk our hides, tryin' to arrest him? Guess again, Cliff. He's a professional-lightnin'-fast. And we ain't as young as we used to be, nor as spry. Blain could cut the both of us down quicker'n you could wink."

"So we don't do nothin'?"

"We wait—and hope."

"Hope the saddlebum wins?"

"You never know," shrugged the sheriff. "Blain might miss."

"I gotta admit I ain't partial to the idea of facin' Wade Blain," mumbled Sandler.

"We'll bunk in the office tonight," Hansbury decided. "Maybe we'll get a bead on Blain from the window."

"With shotguns."

151

"Uh huh. With shotguns. And, if he kills the saddlebum—and we're in back of him—that'll be the best chance we'll ever get."

The taller Texan rose from his bed a few minutes before the sunrise, trudged over to the wash-basin to splash water into his face and pulled on his clothes. While he strapped on his gunbelt, he glanced to the other bed. Larry had not yet come awake; it spoke volumes for his confidence in Stretch's gun-skill. Had two challengers called Stretch out, he would never have quit the hotel alone. Larry would have tagged him. But one proddy dude with a fancy Colt? Woodville Eustace Emerson was more than capable of defending himself against such an adversary.

He left the room quietly, ambled along the corridor and descended the stairs to the lobby. Reaching the street doorway, he half-expected to hear Blain calling to him. But there was no shouted challenge. The street was tomb-quiet in the dawn light, apparently deserted, when he crossed the porch and stepped down to the sidewalk.

He dawdled into the centre of the street, glancing to right and left. Still no sign of Blain. And then, loud and ominous, he heard the gunshot and felt a tugging sensation at his right side. He dropped his gaze, genuinely astonished to discover that his rightside holster had been blown from his belt. It lay in the dust a few feet away, still housing his righthand Colt.

Blain chuckled triumphantly and rose from behind a water trough some 15 yards along the street. He twirled his gleaming six-gun by its trigger-guard, a flashy exhibition of dexterity, then sheathed it smoothly. The handsome face was creased in an arrogant smile, a smile that would have quickly faded had he realised he was being surveyed from a second storey window, from behind Larry's cocked .45.

"I got to admit," drawled Stretch. "That was neat. Yep. Real neat."

"Just so you'll know what you're up against, saddletramp," jeered Blain.

"That's not why you shot his righthand gun away," Larry was thinking. "You figured to give yourself an edge—figured him for a right-hander."

Blain was still grinning, unaware the joke was on him. It happened that, with his matched .45s, the taller Texan was ambidexterous, his right hand no faster than his left.

"And now we're on equal terms," called

153

Blain. "One weapon a piece." He spread his legs slightly and swept back his coat-tails. "And now I'm going to kill you, saddletramp!"

"How d'you know I can't pull just as fast with my left hand?" Stretch asked mildly.

"Make your play!" snarled Blain.

"I ain't in no hurry." Stretch shrugged nonchalantly. "You start, dude. And-uh-I'll try and catch up."

Blain swore luridly. His right hand moved as swiftly as the head of a striking rattler, but a shade slower than Stretch's left. The taller Texan's lefthand gun was out and roaring before Blain could empty his holster, and then the dude was yelling wildly and staggering, his right arm hanging limp and useless, blood-stained from elbow to wrist; his Colt, uncocked, lay in the dust.

"You—scum!" he groaned. "You and—your fool luck . . . !"

"It wasn't luck, mister," retorted Stretch. He fired again. His second bullet neatly whisked Blain's hat away. "Call that luck?" He lowered his barrel and cut loose again, and Blain's fancy Colt leapt out of the dust. While it spun, he triggered a fourth slug and hit it again so that it careered clear to the sidewalk. "That ain't luck," he drawled. "It's a habit."

Blain was flopping to his knees, groaning in anguish and demanding that a doctor be summoned, and Stretch was placidly re-loading, when Larry emerged from the hotel and the two lawmen spilled out of the sheriff's office, both toting shotguns. By the time they reached the wounded gunman and hauled him to his feet, other locals were converging on the scene; the sound of shooting had alerted the early-risers. There were shouted questions and excited comments, as the towners heard Sandler identify Stretch's victim.

"Wade Blain—the killer!"

"It's Wade Blain—and the tall feller busted his gunarm!"

"Let up on that hollerin'!" chided the sheriff. "You—big feller . . ." He gestured to Stretch. "You come along with us. We got business to settle."

"The hell you have," growled Larry, tucking his shirt into his pants. "My partner winged the dude in self-defense."

"That's how it was," Stretch assured them.

"I know," grinned Hansbury.

155

"We seen it," grinned Sandler. "Get movin', Blain. March!"

"A doctor . . . !" raged Blain.

"You'll get doctored in the calaboose," chuckled Sandler.

After the gunman had been installed in a cell, with Sandler standing guard and the local medico tending his wound, Hansbury calmly explained to the Texans,

"Blain was wanted all over—from the Gunnison River country all the way down to Tucson. Robbery and murder. A thousand dollars reward. Only nobody had the nerve to try and collect—on account of his reputation. Guess this is your lucky day, big feller."

"Well-uh . . ." began Stretch.

"Don't give him no arguments," chided Larry. "We can use that thousand. Belle and Nora'll travel a lot easier in some kind of rig."

"I'll make out the claim for the bounty," offered Hansbury. "You sign it and I'll witness it and then all you have to do is wait for the Wilkesville bank to send the money. Might take three days—maybe four . . ."

"We can't wait that long," said Larry.

"We got a little unfinished business," Stretch explained. "Got to move on rightaway."

"All right, we'll go talk to Jake Goldberg soon as the bank opens," offered Hansbury. "Long as Jake knows I'm endorsin' your claim, he'll be glad to advance you the bounty."

On the porch of the hotel, the Texans found Floyd and his sisters awaiting them. Stretch exhibited his rightside holster, grinned wryly and told them,

"I'm gonna have to find a saddler and have him fix a new strap."

"First we eat," said Larry. "Then you can look for a saddler, while I parlay some of that dinero into a rig and team."

When the Rigg sisters left Gillsbury and took to the southwest trail, they were traveling in comfort, sharing the seat of a buckboard drawn by a strong-backed bay, their baggage secured behind, and Floyd and the Texans riding escort. To refuse the $50 bounty offered by Jethro Pinchley and his neighbors had seemed the natural thing to do, considering the near-penury of the farm folk. But bounty on a wanted killer was something else again. This time, Stretch could justly claim he needed the money for a good cause.

They made Arizona three days later, still

unaware of the six hard cases dogging their trail. On the fourth day, they passed a detachment of cavalry, sighted the stockade of the army post away to the east and the clapboard and adobe buildings of the township dead ahead.

As the rig rolled into town with Floyd and the Texans riding abreast, interested locals emerged onto the sidewalks to gape at the beautiful sisters. Especially interested were the men of the town, and the off-duty troopers, and beardless youths and grizzled old timers. The only males unmoved by the sight of the fire-haired beauties on the buckboard seat had not yet reached the age of puberty.

After noting the yearning glances of the girls' new admirers, Larry decided,

"First thing we have to do is get 'em out of sight."

He led the party to a hotel proudly boasting Ladies & Gents Baths, ordered Floyd to check them in and sit guard outside the bathroom door while his sisters rid themselves of three days' accumulated trail-dust.

"You don't budge till Stretch and me show," he stressed.

"But—about Mike . . ." began Floyd.

"We'll do all the askin'," said Larry. "You stick close to Belle and Nora. I got a hunch there's twenty men to every female in Fort Resolution."

"And that," Stretch solemnly opined, "could mean trouble."

The Texans waited to see the Riggs safely into the hotel, then delivered the horses and buckboard to a livery stable and began a canvass of the local saloons.

Several gamblers, saloonkeepers and barkeeps recalled the jaunty Mike Rigg when shown the photograph, but were uncertain as to what had become of him.

"He ain't still here, that's for sure," drawled Stretch, as they approached another saloon.

"Maybe not, but where's the sense of movin' on without one notion where he headed?" countered Larry. "We ought to have *somethin'*—a hunch, a guess, an idea."

At McGarrity's Bar, they got their first lead. McGarrity, a genial Arizonian, proved to be a one-man information bureau. He could remember the accent, the drinking habits and the exact height of his first customer, when he opened this bar eight years before, so recalling the errant Mike to mind was no difficult chore.

"Mike Rigg? Sure, I remember him." He glanced at the picture and nodded emphatically. "Yeah, that's Mike. The short one."

"Now we're gettin' somewhere," remarked Stretch.

"Likable young feller," mused McGarrity. "Wasn't here long. Less than three days, and that was quite a time ago."

"Anything you can remember," urged Larry. "Anything at all."

"Glad to oblige," said McGarrity. "Well now, as I recall, he wasn't real lucky at poker. Guess I taught him a thing or two when him and his buddy and a couple of us professionals had us an all-night game. Oh, he didn't lose his shirt. Matter of fact he ended up a winner. Left the game about seventy bucks richer. His buddy now, *he* was a winner. Started with a two hundred dollar stake, built it to . . ." He paused a moment, his eyes half-closed, "exactly twenty-two hundred and fifty."

"So Mike had a sidekick," frowned Stretch.

"They got along fine, those two," nodded McGarrity. "I was watching when they rode into town, pegged 'em for a couple close friends. Mike headed right here to my place.

160

His pal made straight for the post office, collected a package."

"So they played poker, stayed out of trouble, then quit town," said Larry. "That's all of it?"

"That's all," said McGarrity. "The game was square. Wasn't one angry word. That's how I like it." He took a pull at his bourbon and nodded complacently. "Everything friendly. Sore-heads oughtn't be allowed inside six feet of a poker deck."

"No chance you heard one of 'em mention a name—a town maybe?" prodded Larry. "They didn't say where they were headed next?"

"Sorry," said McGarrity.

"About Mike's sidekick," said Larry.

"Name of Sammy," said McGarrity. "Come to think of it, I never heard his second name. Skinny jasper. A mite close-mouthed, but friendly enough." He half-closed his eyes again. "Got a half-moon scar on his forehead."

The Texans traded grins.

"Left side, right side or smack-dab in the middle?" asked Larry.

"Right side," said McGarrity. "About— three-quarters of an inch above his right eyebrow."

161

"How'd he keep his pants up?" challenged Stretch. "With a belt or suspenders?"

"Can't help you there," frowned McGarrity. "He had his coat on the whole time."

"McGarrity, I thank you kindly," said Larry. "And, if I ever want to know how General Grant likes his eggs, I'll come and ask you."

"Scrambled," grinned McGarrity. "But that's just a guess."

It was noon, when Larry and Stretch rejoined the Riggs. In the hotel dining room they ordered lunch and held a conference, while the other guests tried to digest their food and ogle the beautiful redheads simultaneously. Larry recounted the gist of their conversation with McGarrity, then demanded to be told,

"Just who is this Sammy hombre?"

"Funny—if Mike and him are in cahoots," frowned Floyd.

"You think it could be . . . ?" began Belle.

"Sammy Carr?" asked Nora.

"Well, the description fits," shrugged Floyd. "Except Sammy was never so lucky at poker before." He nodded thoughtfully. "Skinny— with a half-moon scar on his forehead. Sure, that'd have to be Sammy Carr."

"What's funny about Mike sidin' this Sammy?" prodded Stretch.

"They're kind of different," said Floyd. "Sammy's quiet. I always thought he was a mite shifty, but harmless enough. Can't imagine him throwin' in with a rowdy galoot like Mike."

"Mike's not rowdy," chided Nora. "Just—high-spirited."

"I wonder when they met up," mused Floyd. "Near as I can recollect, Sammy used to hang around San Jose about three years ago. Shiftless he was. Never had a regular job. He was gone from the territory before us Riggs flew the coop."

"Maybe they've split up by now," suggested Belle.

"And maybe they haven't," shrugged Larry. "We got no way of knowin'." Their lunch arrived. He dug into his food with his brow creased. Belle, studying him covertly, had never seen him so disgruntled. "When you get right down to it," he growled, "you have to admit we ain't any closer to findin' Mike than when we started out. We've come to a blind end, here in Fort Resolution. All we know is he was here, but a long time back."

163

"We got transportation," Floyd pointed out. "We can keep movin'."

"Keep moving where to?" challenged Nora. "I know what Larry's thinking, and I feel the same way. Where's the sense to traveling from town to town, asking questions and maybe never getting any useful answers?"

"That's how *I* feel," frowned Belle. "But what else can we do? Three of us got together. I don't relish the idea of heading for home until we've found Mike."

Inspiration eluded Larry until he had finished eating and was working on his third refill of coffee. The idea came to him, as he noted the wistful eyes of the male diners, all of them focusing on Belle and her sister.

"This town's got a sheriff and deputy," he said softly. "We passed the law office on our way here. Also, there's a Western Union office."

"So?" challenged Stretch.

"Town looks peaceful," drawled Larry. "Chances are them badge-toters are gettin' lazy. So why don't we put 'em to work?"

"Doin' what?" prodded Floyd.

"Checkin'," said Larry. "Telegraphin' every town inside a couple of hundred miles of Fort

164

Resolution. Askin' all them other lawmen if they've seen Mike—or Sammy. That's what I call a short-cut, a time-saver."

"Hey now," grinned Stretch.

"It's like little Nora said," declared Larry. "No sense wanderin' all over. No sense quittin' this burg till we know where to find him."

"That's the best idea you've had so far," enthused Floyd.

"Tell me something, runt," frowned Stretch. "How're we gonna talk a couple lawmen into doin' all that much for us, sendin' all them messages? 'Scuse me for remindin' you, but badge-toters ain't partial to you and me. Not so you'd notice."

"I wasn't thinkin' of us," grinned Larry. "We'll ask—and then Belle and Nora will plead. You know what I mean? I'm bettin' there ain't a man in this town that wouldn't climb a mountain, wrassle a wild bull or dance on fire barefoot, if Belle or Nora asked him to."

"You-uh-want to use my sisters for bait?" frowned Floyd.

"It sounds kind of sneaky," fretted Nora.

"That's what I like about it!" chuckled Belle. "I was getting to where I wished men wouldn't notice me."

"Me too," smiled Nora.

"But now—maybe we can trade on our looks," said Belle, nodding vehemently. "We won't beg from these lawmen. We'll charm 'em. We'll sweet-talk 'em till they're running around in circles."

"We don't want 'em runnin' around in circles," drawled Larry.

"Only as far as the telegraph office," grinned Stretch.

"I guess this is best," Floyd conceded. "I mean, the law in all those other towns'll sit up and pay attention, when they get messages from other lawmen. They wouldn't pay as much heed if we wired 'em."

"That's my hunch," nodded Larry. "So finish your chow and let's go visit the sheriff."

"We'll melt him," Belle confidently predicted. "We bathed before lunch and . . ."

"You sure smell purty," commented Stretch.

"And we're wearing our prettiest gowns," giggled Nora.

"It ought to work," opined Floyd, "if those badge-toters ain't too old to admire 'em."

"Wouldn't matter if they were ninety and feeble," said Larry. "They'll feel like a couple of young bucks when they sight your sisters."

7

$40 Worth of Dynamite

SHERIFF PIKE DYSART and Deputy Marv Weatherill, unkempt, sour-tempered, irritated by the near century temperature, faced each other across the untidy desk in the untidy law office, heavily involved in their checker game and sparing no thought for law enforcement. When Larry, Stretch and Floyd ambled through the open doorway unannounced, they were curtly invited to vamoose.

"Can't you see we're busy?" scowled Dysart, without raising his eyes. "Scat."

"It's your move, Pike," muttered Weatherill.

"Don't rush me," chided Dysart. He was hefty and balding, uncouth and truculent, and that description also fitted the deputy; they could have been brothers. "If there's one breed that irks me, it's a checker-player with no patience."

"We need your help, Sheriff," said Larry. "Been tryin' to locate a certain party. Figured

167

you'd oblige us by wirin' some of your buddies, you know?"

"If you could telegraph his name and description—say to every town inside a couple hundred miles of here," suggested Floyd.

"You must be loco," jeered Dysart. "You think we can spare time—hangin' around the telegraph office—just because a bunch of drifters get a hankerin' to find some no-account?"

"Well, ladies," Larry called over his shoulder. "I guess it just ain't no use. Sheriff's too busy to help us."

They stood clear of the doorway and, right on cue, Belle and Nora moved in. Weatherill started convulsively. Dysart jerked to his feet so quickly that the board overturned, scattering checkers. The lawmen stared fixedly, glassy-eyed, as the girls hurried across to plead with them. Belle stood an inch from Dysart and lifted a hand to his shoulder, her face raised to his. Nora leaned over Weatherill's chair and spoke huskily, so that he caught the full impact of her cologne—and her proximity.

"You couldn't *mean* it," breathed Belle. "You simply *have* to help us."

"We were counting on you," murmured

Nora. "I declare—if you refuse us now—we won't know who to turn to!" She began slumping against the deputy. "Oh, my! I shall swoon, sister Belle. I just know I shall swoon."

"Poor little sister," sighed Belle. "She pines for our brother. If we don't find him soon . . ." She grasped Dysart's bandana, pulling his face close to hers. "We'd be so *thankful*—so very *thankful* . . ."

"And to think . . ." Larry shook his head sadly. "All it'd take is a few telegraph messages. Well, maybe six or seven."

"Maybe a couple dozen," drawled Stretch.

"As a personal favor—to me?" pleaded Belle.

"Please?" begged Nora. "You have the authority, but we—we're only his sisters—wandering from town to town . . ."

"Pining for our lost brother," said Belle.

Dysart was trembling. Weatherill's face was shiny with sweat. The Texans could not have affected them so—even had they shoved cocked six-guns into their faces.

"Well," shrugged Floyd, "if they just can't spare the time . . ."

"We'll do it!" gasped Dysart. "Who said we wouldn't do it?"

169

"Wouldn't take us but a few hours to send them messages," mumbled Weatherill.

"I mean—anything for a lady," Dysart said shakily. "We—we can't have you gals grievin' for your lost brother, can we now?"

"It's our duty!" asserted Weatherill. "C'mon, Pike! We better hurry!"

He leapt to his feet, reached for his hat and dashed out into the street with his boss in hot pursuit, minus his hat. Belle and Nora smiled smugly at the grinning Texans, while Floyd gestured airly and said,

"And that's how you get results."

"You mean that's how Belle and Nora get results," chuckled Larry. He added, as he sauntered over to seat himself in Dysart's chair, "They'll be back in a minute. Maybe sooner."

"They could send all those messages so quickly?" frowned Nora.

Larry grinned and winked and told her, "Wait and see."

Floyd found chairs for his sisters. Stretch sprawled on the office couch and tipped his hat over his eyes. They waited patiently for exactly two minutes, and then the heavy footsteps sounded on the porch, heralding the return of

170

the lawmen. Dysart and Weatherill stood in the doorway, frowning self-consciously.

"We forgot," grunted Dysart. "We-uh-dunno who to ask about. His name and—and what he looks like."

"And all that," nodded Weatherill.

"Short and stocky," smiled Belle.

"Red hair—just like ours," said Floyd.

"And his name is Michael Rigg," said Nora.

"He might be workin' with a feller name of Carr—Sammy Carr," offered Larry.

"And-uh-how old would your brother be?" asked Dysart.

"He's twenty," said Belle. "And that makes him a little older than sister Nora and a little younger than me."

"We'll start sendin' them wires rightaway," mumbled Weatherill.

"You're so kind," sighed Nora.

"You'll find us at the hotel," drawled Larry. "We'll stay on in Fort Resolution, for as long as it takes you gents to track him."

Two and a half hours later, Dysart and his deputy trudged into the hotel lobby to find the sisters and their escorts relaxing in easy chairs. Nora smiled appealingly. The lawmen appeared disgruntled, but Larry took that as a good sign.

"We found out where he's at—him and Carr," frowned Weatherill.

"I was hopin' it'd take longer," said Dysart. "The answer from Levitt's Ford just came in. We only had to wire five towns." He sighed heavily and fixed a hungry stare on Belle. "I guess this means you'll be movin' on right-away."

"We hate to leave—just when we were getting acquainted," murmured Belle. "But we're that anxious to find our brother."

"Levitt's Ford?" prodded Larry, rising from his chair.

"South," said Dysart. "On the Zuni River, right near the New Mexico border." He heaved another sigh and shrugged resignedly. "I can fix you up with a map. You could make it in two-three days."

"And it's for sure, huh?" asked Stretch.

"It's for sure," nodded Dysart. "Levitt's Ford sheriff identifies Michael Rigg and Samuel Carr as regular citizens of that town. Carr's half-owner of a saloon, the Silver Wheel, and Mike Rigg works for him."

"Glory be," breathed Nora. "It means he stopped wandering. He'll be there when we arrive." She touched Weatherill's hand and

172

started him sweating again. "We're so terribly thankful."

"You *gotta* leave rightaway?" Weatherill asked wistfully.

"I'm sorry," smiled Nora. "But—after I'm gone—will you spare a thought for me?"

The deputy swallowed a lump in his throat and fervently predicted,

"I'll just never forget you."

Larry accompanied the lawmen back to their office, while Floyd and the sisters followed Stretch to the livery stable. A short time later, when Larry bade Dysart farewell and returned to the street, his traveling companions were approaching, Belle driving the buckboard with her sister perched beside her, Stretch and Floyd riding abreast, leading Larry's sorrel. From the side-walks, townmen and troopers forlornly watched the fire-haired beauties pass by. Nora fluttered her fingers to them. Belle blew a kiss to a bent-backed old timer, who promptly straightened up, squared his shoulders and doffed his hat.

"Ready, runt?" called Stretch.

"Ready as I'll ever be," said Larry, as he swung astride his mount. "Let's go."

At intervals during that three-day journey

into East Arizona, their progress was followed with keen interest through Herb Mathews' telescope. The hunters stayed only one hour in Fort Resolution. That was as long as it took to establish that their quarry had pressed on to the south. And they were spared the need to ask questions. Almost the entire male population discussed the red-haired sisters.

"Maybe in the next town," Mathews remarked to his cronies on the morning of the third day. "I got a feelin'."

"That's what you said before Gillsburg," complained Shemp.

"And Fort Resolution," growled Smitty.

"A helluva lotta travelin', Herb," muttered Bannerman. "Just to let daylight through one hombre."

"I call it easy money, and I ain't about to quit," retorted Mathews. "But, any time you feel like pullin' out . . ."

"I'm stayin' with it," Bannerman assured him.

"We're all stayin' with it," declared Cully. "We're in this for an even share of that twenty-five hundred dollars."

"That's better'n four hundred apiece," Shemp pointed out.

"Bueno," grunted Mathews. "So quit your gripin' and let's get movin'."

The six desperadoes caught their first glimpse of the Zuni River and their next sight of their quarry some 90 minutes later, from the summit of a high rise. Mathews dug out his telescope again and scanned the terrain west of the moving rig and the three riders, noting they were moving in that direction.

"Another town," he observed. "They'll make it inside the quarter-hour, the rate they're movin'."

"I don't need that contraption of yours," said Shemp, squinting against the sun-haze. "I see it clear, and the ridge south of it."

"So?" challenged Mathews.

"They don't know me," Shemp pointed out. "What d'you say I tag 'em in? If they find Mike Rigg, they'll be movin' on pretty soon, right?"

"I don't reckon they'd hang around," shrugged Mathews.

"So you take the boys and ride a wide circle round the township," suggested Shemp. "Ford the river and wait for me on that ridge."

Mathews nodded slowly.

"Yeah, all right. But don't make us wait too

long, amigo. Find out if little brother is there —then head for the ridge."

In the late morning, when they passed the western outskirts of Levitt's Ford and hustled the horses along the main stem, the searchers' spirits lifted. Belle and Nora were smiling in eager anticipation. Floyd's face was creased in a broad grin. The Texans found it hard to believe that the children of Robbie and Chloe Rigg had wrangled incessantly during their childhood and youth. Their reunion with the younger brother would be the greatest pleasure they had known since quitting their hometown.

The Silver Wheel Saloon was easily located at the end of the second block, a double-storied edifice occupying a corner position, no more impressive, no humbler than a hundred and one saloons patronized by the Lone Star Hellions in almost two decades of drifting. Freshly painted onto the name-sign was the inscription: Proprietors, S. and M. Carr.

As they reined up, Larry turned in his saddle and nodded encouragingly to Floyd and his sisters.

"End of the line—we hope. Climb down and hustle inside."

"I can hardly wait to . . . !" began Nora.

"You don't have to wait," grinned Stretch. "Go ahead, and I hope he didn't pick today to go fishin'. Be kinda nice if he's right inside."

The girls descended from the buckboard, adjusting their bonnets, flicking dust from their gowns. Floyd dismounted, set his hat at a jaunty angle and took their arms.

"Well . . ." He took a deep breath. "Like Stretch said, we don't have to wait no longer."

The Texans swung down and watched the Riggs climb the steps, cross the porch and enter the saloon. Stretch winked and held up a hand with the first two fingers crossed. They scanned the sunlit street a moment and traded howdies with passers-by, they cocked an ear to the joyful laughter, the wild whoops from the barroom, clear proof that the four Riggs were reunited.

"We'll go in now," Larry decided.

They stepped up to the porch and nudged the batwings open. Floyd beckoned them while pounding the back of a dapper, barrel-chested young man with a shock of fire-red hair, almost striking one of his sisters in the process; the girls were jostling one another in their eagerness to embrace their long-lost brother, half-laughing, half-crying. And, studying this emotional scene, Stretch heaved a sigh. The taller Texan was a sentimentalist at heart.

"Kinda chokes you up, huh runt?"

"You get choked up if you want," shrugged Larry. "I'll settle for a beer."

The bartender and the regular clientele of the Silver Wheel aimed grins at the excited group in the corner, as the Texans ambled across to join them.

"Larry—Stretch—say howdy to our brother Mike," beamed Floyd. "We already told him the big news. Mike, these are the gents Pa hired to find us."

"My pleasure." Mike Rigg offered them his hand and a grin poignantly familiar. Of all Robbie's offspring, the younger son resembled him most. Not in stature nor in features. Just the grin. As he shook their hands, he confided, "This is a big day for Belle and Nora and Floyd and me. We haven't had a good fight since we all got separated."

"There'll be no more scrapping," Belle asserted, "and no more splitting up. We're together again and we're staying together."

"Headed home to San Jose and the old Double R," chuckled Floyd.

"How soon can you be ready to leave with us?" demanded Belle.

"Just as soon as we irrigate," Mike assured her. "We got to drink to Pa's lucky strike, and then I'll pack my grip and . . ."

"You still own a horse?" asked Floyd.

"Damn right," nodded Mike. "Buckskin colt. Won him from a horse dealer a couple weeks back. Wilbur . . ." He called to the barkeep. "Drinks all round! Larry—Stretch—what'll you have?"

They kept the barkeep busy for some ten minutes, the Texans drinking beer and enjoying the results of their labors, the four Riggs reunited at last, jubilantly discussing their future.

Stretch had to raise his voice above the laughter of the brothers and the excited chatter of the sisters, to remark to Larry,

"Near finished, huh runt?"

"How's that?"

"The job. What Robbie hired us for. Near finished. All we gotta do is herd these mavericks back to Double R."

"That's all," agreed Larry. He dug out the map, checked their position. "Easy route from

179

here, it looks like. Straight east across the mountains, then south to San Jose."

"You and Sammy in cahoots—how about that?" Floyd challenged his brother.

"We got along fine," said Mike. "Met up a little while after I started travelin', been together ever since. That Sammy, he sure got the craziest luck. By the time we made Levitt's Ford, he had quite a bankroll. Bought himself a half-share of this saloon, and what d'you suppose he did then? Married the owner. Here she comes now."

A plump blonde in a beaded gown was descending the stairs, nodding in response to Mike's invitation. Her smile was amiable, her demeanor friendly. The Texans doffed their Stetsons.

"Madge, I want you should meet my sisters, and brother Floyd. And that's Larry Valentine and Stretch Emerson, couple friends of ours." Mike went on to announce his father's discovery of gold and his decision to leave Levitt's Ford at once. "Gonna miss you and Sammy, but you can see how it is, Madge."

"Home's where the heart is," mused the blonde. "Sure, I can see how it is. No more debts for the Rigg family, huh? No more hard times." She traded smiles with the sisters. "And a proud day for the old folks, when you're all together again."

"Only thing I'm sorry about," frowned Mike. "I wish I could tell Sammy goodbye—personal, I mean. But we hanker to get started, Madge."

"I'll tell him goodbye for you," she offered. "And, pretty soon, we'll hire another poker-dealer." For the benefit of the newcomers, she explained, "Sammy rode out to the Triple M spread. Got to collect on a gambling debt. He won't be back till around sundown."

"Best boss I ever had, old Sammy," declared Mike. "And a good friend too."

"We'll miss you," said Madge Carr. "But I know Sammy would want you to go home—where you belong." She smiled at the sisters again. "This boy was never meant to ramble. He never stops talking of old times, and his family."

Mike stood up, slid an arm about her waist and kissed her cheek.

"Thanks for everything, Madge. Tell Sammy I'll write."

"You write regular, hear?" she ordered.

"I sure will." He turned toward the stairs. "Won't take me but a few minutes to pack my grip. Hey, Floyd, how about you hustle along to the livery and saddle up for me? Buckskin colt at Berkmire's Barn—just a little way downtown."

"That critter'll be ready by the time you find your other shirt," promised Floyd, hurrying to the entrance.

A short time later, when the Riggs emerged from the saloon with the Texans in tow, the lynx-eyed Shemp was watching from a nearby alleymouth. His pulse quickened as the second brother appeared and, for a moment, he gripped the butt of his holstered Colt, an instinctive reaction.

"From here, it'd be dead easy. Put a slug through his head, and it's finished. But this ain't the place. No chance of a getaway."

He retreated into the alley and got mounted. Outside the saloon, Mike tossed his valise onto the buckboard. Stretch lashed it to the other baggage while the brothers helped their sisters aboard. Belle gathered the reins as the men swung into their saddles, and gaily announced,

"Next stop the Double R ranch."

"Double R Cattle and Mining Company," corrected Floyd.

"After a couple night-camps," drawled

Larry. He grinned wryly and asked, "Didn't you Riggs ever hear of sleep?"

By the time the four riders and the buckboard were clearing the river town's outskirts, Shemp was hightailing it across the flats to rendezvous with his cronies atop the ridge. They signaled him when he started up the slope, and he veered left making for the brush-clump where the five awaited him.

Mathews was using his telescope again. As Shemp dismounted, he muttered,

"They found him in that burg, right?"

"That's him," nodded Shemp. "Fancy Dan on the white buckskin."

"Sometime tomorrow, I reckon," opined Mathews, noting the direction taken by the travelers. "Yeah. They're headed for the high country. There'll be a trail, and we'll find it a damn sight faster than they will."

"We got this ridge 'tween us and them," offered Cully.

"Uh huh," grunted Mathews. "They won't be expectin' trouble—and Mike Rigg will never know what hit him. All we gotta do is get well and truly ahead of 'em and find us a stakeout. Tomorrow mornin' we finish it. They have to stay on the trail, on account of that buckboard."

"Short reunion." Bannerman chuckled callously.

"Mount up," ordered Mathews. "If we move fast enough, we could make the foothills before they pass the west end of the ridge."

Sammy Carr returned to Levitt's Ford some two hours earlier than expected. Slight of build, rarely energetic, he wasn't the outdoors type. He hadn't enjoyed the ride to Triple M and back.

"But it was worth it," he assured his wife, joining her at a table near the bar. "Bassett paid up. I knew I could count on him." He poured himself a stiff shot of bourbon, took a pull at it, then glanced toward the gaming tables. "Where's Mike?"

"We've lost him," she smiled. "He's gone from Levitt's Ford, headed for home. But I'm sure you'll understand, Sammy, when I tell you about . . ."

"Mike's—headed back to San Jose?" gasped Carr.

She eyed him in sudden alarm, noting his

pallor. His hand trembled as he lifted his glass and gulped another mouthfull.

"Any reason why he shouldn't?" she frowned. "What're you fretting about, Sammy? I know we were all good friends together and he was getting to be a better than average poker-dealer, but you'll soon hire another man."

"He can't do it," he breathed. "Mike can't go back—*daren't* go back!"

"They came for him."

"Who? Who came for him?"

"No need to grab my arm, honey. You're bruising me."

"Tell me, Madge, for pity's sake!"

"His brother and sisters, and a couple of Texans hired by Old Man Rigg. Seems the old man struck it rich."

"What . . . ?"

"Gold—right there on his own land. So now the Rigg family can afford to live together again. The kids are headed home to help the old folks mine the claim. You can't blame Mike. It's only natural he'd want to . . ."

"When did they leave?" he demanded. And, to her astonishment, he got to his feet and barked a command to the barkeep. "Wilbur,

185

take my horse to the livery and tell Berkmire to saddle another—the fastest animal he owns. Get a move on!" The barkeep hurried away. Carr drained his glass and gestured impatiently. "Well?"

"They didn't wait to eat—too excited I guess," she frowned. "It was around noon when they left. Maybe ten after."

"Damn and blast," he groaned. "They'll be half-way to the foothills by now!"

"You're not thinking of going after them?" she challenged.

"Got to, Madge." He nodded vehemently. "He's entitled to a warning. I owe him that much."

"I don't understand."

"Maybe I'll explain it when I get back. Can't wait now, Madge. His time's running out." Carr started for the stairs, then paused and stared morosely toward the batwings. "The hell of it is—he doesn't *know*."

"I never saw you this way before," she murmured.

"I never *felt* this way before," he retorted. "You're looking at a smart-aleck opportunist, Madge." He returned to her for a moment, dropping a hand to her shoulder. "A chiseller with a conscience."

"You keep talking in riddles," she complained.

"Two things I want you to believe," he said earnestly. "Marrying you was the best thing ever happened to me. I'll never even look at another woman. That's one thing . . ."

"And the other?" she asked.

"Going after Mike—warning him," said Carr, "will be the first real kindness I've done for him since we joined up." He laughed mirthlessly. "Imagine me—turning soft! It seems I'm not the two-timing chiseller I thought I was."

He hurried upstairs. When he descended to the barroom again, his wife was startled to observe he had strapped on his gunbelt. He kissed her and, without another word, strode out to the street and the saddled horse fetched by the barkeep.

Following the trail to the foothills, he scanned the terrain ahead, his mind troubled, his bones and muscles aching a protest against this unwelcome activity. Fast riding was not exactly Sammy Carr's idea of a good time; he preferred an upholstered chair at a poker table. At his first pause, to give his rented mount a

187

chance to catch its wind, he studied the surface of the trail.

"An experienced tracker would know if those wheelruts and hoofprints were fresh," he reflected. "For all I know, they could've been made days ago." He studied the tracks carefully. "I make it four riders and a rig—drawn by one horse. All right, Mike. You'd better pray I find you in time."

Moving through the foothills in the late afternoon, his attention was distracted by a flash far to the east. High, up there in the peaks, the sun was reflected on something with a shiny surface. A rifle-barrel? Field-glasses maybe? A chill gnawed at his spine as he urged his mount to greater speed.

He was close to panic at sundown, realizing it would soon be too dark for him to follow the clear sign on the mountain trail. The gloom seemed to close in on him, as he put his horse to another steep grade. Anxiously, he probed the timbered rises, the crags and mounds soaring like grotesque sentinels. And then, with a sigh of relief, he spotted the distant glow. If that were a campfire—their campfire . . .

The travelers had made themselves comfortable in the shelter of a massive rock-shelf. Belle

188

and her sister had rustled up a supper that won the hearty approval of their brothers and the nonchalant Texans, both very much at their ease, anticipating an unhurried, uneventful journey through the mountains and south to San Jose. Stretch had picketed the horses. Now, they socialized with Robbie Rigg's reunited offspring and did justice to their share of a fine supper.

Larry was first to hear the approaching horseman. He nodded to Stretch and dropped a hand to his holster. The taller Texan rose and sauntered beyond the firelight.

"You gents always so jumpy?" grinned Mike.

"Not jumpy, young feller," drawled Larry. "Just cautious."

"When you been on the drift as long as we have," Stretch muttered, "it gets to be a habit."

The voice reached them then, and Mike grinned broadly.

"Mike? That you, Mike . . . ?"

"It's Sammy!" chuckled Mike. "Old son-ofagun must've tagged us all the way from Levitt's Ford. Hey, Sammy! Over here!"

Carr trudged into view, leading his horse. The Texans relaxed. Floyd frowned per-plexedly, noting Carr's haggard visage, his haunted eyes. Stretch relieved him of his rein and led his horse across to where the other animals were tethered.

"Heck, Sammy, you didn't have to . . ." began Mike.

"Yes," Carr nodded grimly. "Yes, I had to."

He squatted crosslegged beside Floyd, nodding a greeting as Mike introduced his relatives and the Texans, seemingly oblivious to the beautiful sisters. When Belle passed him a cup of coffee, he mumbled his thanks.

"Well, for gosh sakes, Sammy boy," chided Mike. "This is no funeral party. You don't have to act so mournful. Didn't Madge tell you? The Riggs are rich. We're goin' home to help Pa run a gold mine."

Carr fumbled in his pockets, found a cigar and got it working. Suddenly, he was calm, resigned to the inevitable. In a little while, some of these people would be eyeing him in cold scorn, probably voicing their contempt. But he could endure that. His conscience would be clear for the first time in years.

"Sammy, old pal," frowned Mike. "What's ailin' you? You look like a panhandler caught with his paw in somebody else's pocket."

"Don't call me 'pal'," muttered Carr.

190

"You sick or somethin'?" prodded Larry. "I could boost your coffee with a slug of rye."

"I'd be obliged," Carr said softly. "Yeah, do that for me. And then I'll say my piece—and you won't feel like buying me a drink again."

Larry frowned at Stretch, who unearthed a bottle from his saddlebag. They spiked Carr's coffee. He swigged a couple of mouthfuls and, with his eyes downcast, began a confession,

"I couldn't let you head home to San Jose, Mike. You show your face in your old hometown and, pretty soon, somebody's gonna take a shot at you. I'm warning you to turn back."

"But—that's crazy," protested Mike. "I got no enemies in San Jose—leastways nobody that'd want to kill me."

"What on earth . . . ?" began Belle.

"Easy," grunted Larry. "This jasper's totin' quite a load . . ."

"Of guilt," scowled Carr.

"That's what I figured," nodded Larry. "You got that look about you." Eyeing the others warningly, he suggested, "Let's hear it all."

"Don't worry," sighed Carr. "I wasn't planning on telling the half of it. You'll hear it all." He took another pull at his reinforced coffee, another drag at his cigar, then worked up the

191

courage to look directly at Mike. "Don't ever call me 'pal' again. I've been using you, boy. Yeah, right from the start."

"Usin' me?" challenged Mike. "How?"

"I had information," muttered Carr. "When I quit San Jose, I knew a thing or two about five well-heeled citizens. And I figured on making those buzzards pay for my silence."

"Blackmail," said Larry.

"You named it right," nodded Carr. "But I was leery. Couldn't figure a *safe* way. I wanted their cash—but no risks attached. They had to believe I knew what I know, but I needed a fall guy. And, when I met up with Mike, I thought I had it made. The best chance I'd ever get. So I stuck close to him—and sent off the first letters." He grinned wryly. "Remember all those towns we passed through, on our way to Levitt's Ford?"

"I remember," said Mike. "There was always a package waitin' for you."

"I never demanded big amounts," said Carr. "Just a couple hundred—at irregular intervals. And—I signed your name to every letter I sent to those killers. I made 'em mail the cash to post offices all over, gave 'em a different name every time, but always signed your name to the letters. At Fort Resolution, I picked up two hundred addressed to K. P. Jorgenson. Remember how we took that poker party in McGarrity's Bar? And all those other towns— packages for John Wallace and T. J. Zimmerman and Rufus McCord. Boy, I never ran short of names. But the name that mattered most was the name I signed when I demanded another pay-off. Your name, Mike. My insurance. If they ever caught up with you, I'd be safe. You'd end up with a bullet that should've been triggered at me." He paused, feeling the full impact of Belle's accusing stare and the Texans' grim silence. "Go ahead, kid. Spit in my face. Clobber me. You sure got a right."

"You haven't told it all, Sammy," frowned Mike. "You haven't said why you changed your mind—why you rode all this way to warn me."

"Plain enough, isn't it?" shrugged Carr. "At the start, I didn't care a damn what happened to you. I was looking out for Number One— Smart Sammy. But we traveled quite a ways together, kid. By the time we made Levitt's Ford and I started courting Madge, you and me were old buddies. I'd gotten into the habit of trusting you. And you always trusted me."

"Guilt," said Larry, "plays strange tricks."

"That's about the size of it," muttered Carr. "I got to likin' Mike. He was my best man when I married Madge. I haven't sent a letter to any of those polecats in San Jose for quite a time. We had everything we ever wanted, a good business, Madge and me all settled down. I figured I'd been greedy enough and I ought to forget the whole lousy deal. But today, when Madge told me you were headed home, I knew it wasn't over. I couldn't let you ride into San Jose again—a target for any one of 'em, or all five."

"Sonofagun," breathed Mike.

"Go ahead," urged Carr. "Let me have it right in the face. I got it coming."

Mike frowned uncertainly at his brother and sisters, all of them silent, stunned by Carr's declaration. Not so Larry. He wanted to know more, and said so.

"Who are they?" he demanded.

"Bonner and his partner," said Carr. "McMurtrie and Rusk that run the general store. And Mayor Garbutt."

"Well, well, well," grinned Stretch. "I guess we remember *them*, huh runt?"

"What've you got on 'em?" frowned Larry.

194

"It adds up to a mighty dirty story," warned Carr. "The ladies . . ."

"Don't mind us," Belle said gruffly.

"You called 'em killers," Larry reminded him.

"Not the mayor," said Carr. "I don't think that lard-bellied cheater could work up the nerve to kill anybody. But Bonner for sure." He hesitated a moment. "You have to understand. I mean, back when these things happened, we were all prospecting, trying to get a start . . ."

"I'd forgotten you once had a claim," said Mike.

"Well, I never struck gold, and neither did Bonner nor his sidekick, that Marco feller," said Carr. "But they had a friend, old feller name of Joe Kyle, and *he* struck it rich. Worked his claim for all it was worth until there wasn't one ounce of pay-ore left. He had it ready for loading his mules—when Bonner and Marco killed him."

"How'd you know . . . ?" began Stretch.

"I saw it." Carr winced at the memory. "It was too late for me to help Kyle. I was about to lead my horse out of the timber close by, when I saw Bonner shove a knife in Kyle. And

195

—Kyle couldn't defend himself—because Marco was holding his arms."

He paused again. Larry grimaced impatiently.

"Tell it all, mister."

"I sneaked away," mumbled Carr. "I wasn't toting a gun and I figured, if they knew I'd seen them, they'd have to kill me." He shrugged helplessly. "Well, that's how Bonner and Marco got their start. I guess they toted that gold to their own claim and made like *they'd* hit a pay-vein. Don't know how they got rid of the body. But, inside a month, they had what they wanted. The Rialto Saloon—open for business."

"McMurtrie and Rusk?" prodded Larry.

"They robbed the Santa Fé stage," said Carr. "That's how they got cash enough to start their emporium." Anticipating the next question, he explained, "I was a passenger on that stage. They were masked, but I knew one of 'em was McMurtrie. He only has half of the third finger on his left hand."

"Sammy always was sharp-eyed," mused Mike.

"And the mayor?" frowned Floyd. "What about him?"

196

"I thought *everybody* knew." Carr grinned mirthlessly. "But I guess it's still a tight secret. All the property he collects rent on—he doesn't own it. It's all in his wife's name. Lena Garbutt holds the purse strings, if you get what I mean. And she'd get rid of him damn quick—divorce him for sure—if she knew about him and Ruby Hewlett."

"The singin' woman at the Rialto?" blinked Mike.

"So they all paid off," reflected Larry. "The mayor, Bonner and his partner, McMurtrie and Rusk. And they all think they've been payin' Mike."

"Sammy's right about one thing," Floyd said grimly. "Mike don't dare show his face in San Jose. His life wouldn't be worth a bent dime."

8

Dead End in a Ghost Town

AT Larry's insistence, the Riggs rummaged in their baggage and unearthed writing materials. Mike found paper, Nora a pencil. Too intimidated to refuse Larry's demand, Carr wrote down all he had told them about the blackmail victims. He signed the statement, then eyed Larry apprehensively.

"What'll you do with that?" he asked. "Hand it over to the marshal?" He shrugged and bowed his head. "Yeah, I guess you'll have to. And they jail blackmailers."

"Do we have to do it that way?" Mike challenged.

"Up to you, boy," frowned Larry. "You're the one he used. But, if you want to give him a break . . ."

"He didn't have to ride out here and warn me," said Mike.

"You got a point there," agreed Floyd. "I

198

guess we ought to be good and mad at Sam. But, like you say . . ."

Stretch contributed an opinion.

"Any hombre that blackmails five sneakin' coyotes and uses his pard's name to save his own hide and then gets religion and admits he was a sharper and a lousy double-crosser—can't be all bad."

"How's that again?" blinked Floyd.

"Don't ask him to say it again," scowled Larry. "I don't believe he could." He stared hard at Mike. "Well?"

"I don't want to make trouble for Sammy," frowned the younger brother. "We had some good times together, Sammy and me." He shrugged uncomfortly. "All right, so I ought to be sore. But I'm not. So—can't we keep him out of this mess?"

"Depends," said Larry.

"On what?" asked Belle.

"Not on what," countered Larry. "On who. Meanin' Bonner and the others. They have to be taken care of—so they'll never get a chance to hurt Mike."

"Like, for instance, blowin' my head off," growled Mike.

"If they're taken alive, they're bound to hit

back at Mike," Larry pointed out. "They'll claim he was blackmailin' 'em—and you know what that means."

"I know what it means," muttered Carr. "Well, you got my confession—written and signed. If the law wants me, I'll be waiting in Levitt's Ford." He rose to his feet and declared, "I'm going back and tell Madge everything."

"Go ahead, Sammy," nodded Mike. "Nobody's stopping you." Carr eyed him wistfully, as he offered his hand. "Shake—you old two-timer. And tell Madge hallo for me."

Carr gripped his hand a moment, then nodded apologetically to the sisters.

"Before I head back, I got something else to tell you," he announced. "I'm sorry the ladies have to hear it. I don't want to frighten them. And maybe there's no cause for alarm. But you ought to know about it—just in case."

"Now what?" demanded Stretch.

"It could be you're headed into an ambush," said Carr. "I mean here in the high country." He gestured eastward. "Up there in the peaks, I saw the sun flash on something when I was traveling through the foothills. Mightn't mean anything. On the other hand . . ."

200

"A stakeout?" Stretch glanced at Larry. "What d'you think?"

"I think we better not take no chances," Larry said thoughtfully. "A lot of people knew Robbie hired us to find his young'uns. Bonner had to hear of it."

"So maybe he did a little hirin'?" prodded Stretch.

"Or maybe he plans on handlin' this chore personal," drawled Larry. "Like Carr says, Mike only means one thing to Bonner and his pards. Trouble. And that makes him a target."

"Up to the peaks," Carr repeated, "three—maybe four miles." He eyed Mike a moment, then forced himself to meet the intent gaze of the other redheads. Humbly he told them, "For what it's worth—I'm sorry."

He trudged to his horse, untethered it and swung astride. Mike grinned encouragingly and lifted a hand in farewell, as he rode away from the shelf and back to the mountain trail. The brief silence that followed was broken by Floyd, asserting his authority as elder brother.

"All right now, we got to make plans," he said briskly. "Got to figure how we're gonna get Mike home safe, without a run-in with Bonner and his pards."

"One thing at a time, Floyd," muttered Larry. He nodded to Stretch, and the taller Texan began readying the pinto and the sorrel. "First we check the route you'll be travelin' manana. Maybe Bonner set up an ambush and maybe he didn't. We aim to make sure, either way."

"You'll scout ahead," guessed Belle.

"Join up with you in the mornin'," nodded Larry. "You girls get your sleep. You'll be movin' on at first light. Meantime Mike and Floyd takes turns to set guard. And stay sharp, understand?"

"As if you need to tell us," frowned Mike.

"Floyd owns a rifle," Larry recalled. "How about you?"

"Six-gun in my saddlebag," said Mike. "Don't worry. I'm handy enough with a Colt, when I have to be."

"Well—uh what's the plan?" demanded Floyd. "How about signals? How far do we go?"

"You just get movin' right after breakfast," ordered Larry. "Keep pushin' east along the regular trail, slow and steady. If you hear shootin', stall the rig, get Belle and Nora to cover and stay with 'em. And don't budge till one of us comes for you. That's all you have to remember. You got it?"

"Got it," nodded Floyd.

"You were hired to find us and escort us home," Belle murmured. "Does that include— risking your lives on our account?"

"Don't fret about it," grinned Larry.

"It's a habit," grunted Stretch.

By midnight, the trouble-shooters had climbed far east of the campsite, sticking to the mountain trail for the first two miles, then cutting away some 60 yards to the south to ride a hogsback. From that elevated position, the trail was clearly visible; it was a night of bright moonlight and the wind blew from the east.

Mathews and his unsavory crew were showing no light. Huddled in their ponchos and blankets, they squatted behind a semi-circle of boulders on a rise overlooking a bend of the trail, some of them catnapping, some too cold —or over-stimulated—for sleep. They cursed the chill of the night, but grudgingly conceded it would have been unwise to light a fire, a beacon to betray their position.

Had the Texans begun their scout a quarter-hour earlier, they might have encountered

203

Mathews, who had checked a fair stretch of the terrain west.

"Saw their camp," he told Shemp. "They're quite a ways off, and that's okay by me." He grinned coldly. "I can be patient. They have to come this way—the only route for a rig."

"They'll be on the move again come sun-up," Shemp predicted.

Cully stirred in his blankets, groaning a curse.

"You galoots gonna gab all night?" he challenged.

"Shuddup and quit your gripin'," leered Mathews. "After tomorrow mornin', it'll all be over. We'll be headed back to Nueva Fortuna to set up a meetin' with Bonner."

"What about—the rest of 'em?" frowned Shemp. "Big brother—and them tall jaspers?"

"We got the edge." Mathews shrugged unconcernedly. "They try for a shot at us and what can they see from down there on the trail? Just these rocks and our gun-barrels."

"Yeah, all right," nodded Shemp. "We got 'em outnumbered anyway."

"And then some," chuckled Mathews. He stopped laughing as a match flared. "Damn you, Smitty, put out that light!"

"Aw, hell . . ."

"I said no smokin'! Put it out!"

"They ain't gonna see . . ."

"We take no chances! Get rid of the stogie, you damn fool! You scratch another match and, so help me, I'll break every bone in your no-good carcass!"

The would-be smoker swore luridly and returned matches and cigars to his pockets.

Hunched low in their saddles at the near end of the ridge, staring intently to the east, the Texans held a muttered council of war.

"You see it?" challenged Larry.

"Just for a second," nodded Stretch. "Match-flare, nothin' surer." He grinned crookedly. "Mighty obligin' of 'em, huh?"

"Somebody made a fool mistake," opined Larry. "And, if he's part of an ambush party, it's gonna cost him."

"Over thataway," offered Stretch, gesturing. "High rise."

"Yeah. I see it." Larry scanned the slope below. "We'll scout afoot, after we get these critters to low ground. Easy now. No hustlin'. If they hear our horses, we lose our chance to take 'em by surprise."

They made a slow descent from the ridge and

dismounted on soft ground, then led their horses to the concealment of a clump of trees. There, they hobbled the animals, unsheathed and readied their Winchesters and filled their pockets with spare shells.

It took them until the hour before dawn to find a stakeout ideal for their purpose—a counter-action, in the event the men atop the bend proved hostile. The soaring mound of lava-rock appeared unscalable until they made the attempt, and that dangerous climb won them a vantagepoint, a niche just deep enough to accommodate them, huddled side by side with their weapons dipped toward the rise 45 yards away and slightly below.

They now commanded a clear view of the ambush party. The only cover on the summit of the rise was the semi-circle of boulders at its west edge. Mathews and his men would be invisible from the trail, but were in clear view of the Texans. The six horses were hobbled half-way down the east slope.

"I make it six," muttered Stretch. "And— you should pardon if I mention—we're like a couple of flies on a wall."

"Stay low, shoot straight and hope for the best," frowned Larry.

"How long do we wait?"

"Till there's light enough for us to draw clear beads. If those hombres are peaceable, there'll be no shootin'."

"But—if they're here to stunt Mike's growth —permanent?"

"We'll know it. We'll find out—right after I challenge 'em."

They endured the chill of early morning with their customary stoicism, watching the hard cases rouse, roll from their blankets and make their preparations. Some emptied holsters and checked pistols. Some readied rifles. Bannerman toted the packrolls down to where the horses were hobbled, tagged by Cully. They tied the gear to saddles and rejoined their cohorts. Mathews was on his feet now, warily scanning the trail.

"Light enough?" grunted Stretch.

"Light enough," nodded Larry. "Better pick yourself a target. If they get to shootin', we can't afford to give 'em any kind of chance."

"Them or us," Stretch said grimly. "Yeah. That's what I was thinkin'." He studied the ambushers carefully. "I don't see Bonner or any of his buddies—don't see anybody I've seen before."

"They could've been sent here by Bonner," retorted Larry. "Anyway—we're about to find out." He lined his rifle on Mathews. "Ready?"

"Born ready," said Stretch. "Start hollerin'."

Larry's bellowed challenge echoed across the peaks and won a violent reaction.

"If you jaspers are plannin' on ambushin' the Riggs—forget it! We got you surrounded!"

Quint and Smitty scrambled to their feet, their Colts at the ready. Mathews loosed a shocked oath and scanned the area in sudden panic, while Shemp swung his rifle toward the mount; he had marked the Texans' position.

"Up there!" he yelled.

As he leveled his rifle, Larry squeezed the trigger. The impact of the .44.40 slug sent Shemp reeling back to collide with Mathews, and then Quint and Smitty were emptying their guns in a savage but futile burst and Bannerman was snarling defiance, his rifle barking in crackling unison with Cully's. Bullets slammed into the grit bare inches above the Texans' heads, as they got their Winchesters working, raking the stakeout, triggering a lethal hail at the moving figures.

Bannerman flopped with his right arm bloody, his face contorted. As Mathews nudged

Shemp's body away and leapt up to level his rifle, he heard Cully's dying yell and an anguished cry from Quint, who dropped his Colt and clasped a hand to his side.

"Herb—it's no good!" wailed Bannerman. "We can't . . . !"

His plea was drowned by the barking of Mathews' rifle, and then that weapon was silenced. A well-aimed slug from Stretch's Winchester mortally wounded the flabby hard case; he was dead before he hit ground.

"Hold your fire," grunted Larry. "They're pullin' out."

Smitty, as yet unscathed, dropped to his knees beside Mathews' body and emptied his pockets. He dashed after Quint and Bannerman, who were lurching drunkenly down the slope toward their horses. In panic, but slowed down by their wounds, the survivors struggled to get mounted. Smitty swung astride his horse, making no effort to help them.

"If you're comin' . . . !" he began.

"You grabbed the dinero—we seen you!" groaned Quint, as he pulled himself into his saddle.

"Wait for us—for pity's sakes!" begged Bannerman.

"We're headin' north!" yelled Smitty. "The hell with waitin' for the Riggs. I've had enough!"

Grim-faced, the Texans watched the three riders flee the scene of their bitter defeat, Bannerman and Quint barely able to stay mounted.

"We climb down now," muttered Larry. "I'll start plantin' the losers where they fell, while you head back to the horses and go fetch the young'uns."

They made the tricky descent without mishap and separated, Stretch moving back to the trees, Larry making for the slope of the rise, trudging up to inspect the three sprawled bodies. He was beginning the graves, scooping with his bare hands and with his improvised spade, the sharp end of a sapling, when the buckboard approached the bend, led by Stretch and the brothers. From the rocks, he signaled the men to come on, firmly gesturing for the girls to stay put. Solemn and subdued, the sisters stayed on the buckboard seat, while their brothers followed Stretch up to the summit of the rise.

"We heard the shootin'," muttered Floyd.

"Held back just like you told us," frowned Mike. "But I got to admit we hankered to come

210

on and lend a hand." He moved across to the dead men and studied the contorted faces. Floyd joined him, shook his head and mouthed an oath. "Strangers, huh?"

"Never saw 'em before," said Floyd. "Larry —were you sure?"

"Don't waste any sympathy on 'em," growled Larry. "They were staked out and waitin' for you."

"Old Sammy . . ." Mike sighed heavily. "He sure wasn't foolin'. He said Bonner and his friends would try to kill me—and he wasn't foolin'." He peeled off his coat and nodded to his brother. "Come on. The least we can do is help bury these jaspers."

By the time they were moving on along the mountain trail, headed for the eastern foothills and the turn-off to San Jose, the mood of the travelers had changed. The Rigg redheads, so jubilant the night before, filled with optimism and glad to be together again, were grim-faced and silent, Belle bitterly indignant, Nora shocked to the core.

While they were noon-camped below the last slope, staring toward the sprawling prairie south, Stretch eyed his partner expectantly and put words to the thought in all their minds.

"Bonner hired guns to stop the kid. We took care of 'em—but we didn't change anything."

"That's right. Nothin's changed." Larry frowned moodily at the steam rising from his coffee. "He's still a target. No peace for him—for any Rigg—until we settle Bonner's hash."

"We're headed home—but it just isn't *safe* to head home," frowned Belle. "When Bonner learns of Mike's return . . ."

"Well, consarn 'em, are we gonna let 'em keep us out of San Jose?" challenged Floyd. "We gonna stick here and fret?"

"Give Larry a little time," advised Stretch. "He'll think of somethin'."

"And while he's thinkin'," complained Mike, "I'm cravin' to see home again, the old Double R." He forked up another mouthful of beans and scowled resentfully. "That's where we belong. We ought never have quit."

"They need us," said Floyd. "Pa and Ma."

They finished eating. The sisters packed the cooking gear, while the brothers watched Larry, impatiently awaiting his decision. Stretch kicked dirt onto the fire. Larry began talking again, quietly, thoughtfully.

"Here's how it adds up. If we ride right into San Jose, there's a better than even chance we'd run into a shootin' fight with Bonner and his friends. And let's not forget Bonner can scare up some more help—his hard case crew from the Rialto."

"Includin' Shotgun Farley," scowled Floyd.

"If we head straight for Double R and deliver you kids to the old folks, Bonner'll get to hear of it sooner or later," Larry went on. "And I don't think Marshal Noad could stop Bonner. There'd be a raid on Double R."

"Nothin' surer," agreed Stretch.

"Well, damnitall, we can't let *that* happen," asserted Mike. "There'd be danger for Ma and Pa and the girls."

"So," shrugged Larry, "that leaves me with just one notion—and I like it fine. Instead of ridin' right into a showdown with Bonner and his friends . . ." He stood beside his sorrel, rolling a cigarette and grinning wryly, "We make them come to us."

"Hey now!" chuckled Stretch.

"And we'll be waitin' for 'em, loaded for bear," drawled Larry.

"That's a helluva notion and, by golly, we'll go along with it," declared Mike. "Right, Floyd?"

"Right," grinned Floyd.

"Come to us?" challenged Belle. "Come to us—where?"

"Good question," said Larry. "All right, you Riggs know that territory better than us. Any ideas?"

The sisters climbed to the buckboard seat. Belle took the reins and frowned at her brothers, who mounted slowly, their brows wrinkled in thought. Stretch swung astride the pinto and tossed Larry his matches. Larry lit up, returned the vestas and raised a boot to stirrup, remarking,

"Some place well clear of San Jose, where no neutrals could stop a bullet. And we'll need safe cover for Belle and Nora."

The brothers traded quick glances.

"Nueva Fortuna?" breathed Mike.

"The old ghost town." Floyd nodded eagerly. "Couldn't be a better place for it." To the Texans he explained, "It's empty. Everybody knows about it—and stays away from it. There's some fools thinks it's haunted."

"Runt, what d'you think?" asked Stretch.

"Ghost town'd have everything we need," opined Larry. "Yeah. It better be Nueva Fortuna. How far from here, Floyd?"

"Once we're on the south trail, I'd say we'd

make Nueva Fortuna day after tomorrow," Floyd calculated. "It's north of San Jose. We'd get there in the early mornin', day after tomorrow, if we hustle."

"So," said Larry, "we hustle."

The only being haunting Nueva Fortuna was elderly and human, a lone-wolf prospector, Ike Bosely by name, who had never abandoned the hope of making a strike in the ghost town. Few travelers had ventured in since the original settlers departed, leaving Nueva Fortuna to the mercy of the elements. Mathews and his crew had established a temporary headquarters here, and Ike had stayed clear of them. Once, he had been spotted by Cully, and had thrown a bad scare into that hard case by crawling over a roof in the pallid moonlight in his duster, his head covered by a hood improvised from a floursack. The desperadoes had shown no inclination to seek out the "ghost".

Ike wondered if the approaching travelers would scare so easily. Too late for him to avoid them. They must have seen the smoke rising from the chimney of his shack on the edge of the abandoned settlement; he was cooking his breakfast when the buckboard and riders

215

appeared, moving in from the north. Old, but by no means senile, his ash-grey hair hanging to his shoulders, his beard ending down near his third shirt button, the loner was a peace-lover with a deep-rooted antipathy for trouble-makers.

"Got to admit they don't look like trouble," he reflected. "Two purty gals in the buckboard. Yup. Purty as paint. And a couple of them riders looks a mite familiar."

He hesitated a moment, then stepped out into the sunlight. The travelers came on steadily, heading for the dusty, tumbleweed-littered strip that had once rejoiced in the title: Calle Principal, Main Street, Nueva Fortuna. As they passed, two of the riders greeted him by name. The other two nodded affably and the beautiful redheads on the buckboard seat flashed radiant smiles, causing his heart to skip and his pulse to quicken.

"Howdy, old Ike!" called Floyd. "How you been?"

"Good to see you, old timer," grinned Mike.

The loner nodded uncertainly, watched the newcomers rein up outside the dilapidated Fortuna Saloon, then ambled toward them, his curiosity aroused.

"Ike Bosely—old fossicker," muttered Floyd, as he dismounted beside the Texans. "Don't sell him short."

"He ain't loco—not by a long chalk," Mike declared. "And, come to think of it, he totes a grudge against the Rialto bunch. Bonner had Shotgun Farley throw him out of there one night—just to amuse his customers."

"Unload the baggage and the girls," frowned Larry. "Let's get inside."

The Texans tethered their mounts to the rickety hitch-rail and climbed to the porch. Gingerly avoiding the sagging and splintered boards, they stepped across to the entrance and through to the barroom. When the Riggs joined them with the aged prospector in tow, they were standing by the bar, scanning the shambles of what had once been the noisy retreat of hard-drinking miners and sharp-eyed gamblers, and noting the signs of more recent occupation, a litter of cigar-stubs, matches, discarded bottles.

Mike introduced the loner, explaining, "Nueva Fortuna is still home to him. He's afeared we want to stay on."

"No chance of that, old timer," Larry

declared. "I figure we'll be gone inside of twenty-four hours."

"Ike's no friend of Bonner," Floyd reminded him.

"But them galoots that was bunkin' here a little while back," scowled Ike. "They was in cahoots with Bonner."

"You know that for sure?" challenged Larry.

"They had a visitor, same night they up and quit," said Ike. "I recognized him. Marco. Bonner's sidekick."

"So we can guess who they were," muttered Stretch. "Same bunch tried to pull that ambush."

"You could make book on it," said Larry.

He studied the old man intently, sizing him up, wondering if he could be trusted. As though reading his mind, Floyd said,

"Ike could deliver a message. And he'd do it right."

"Young feller says you'd make it worth my time," frowned the prospector.

"I'll tell you what to say and do," suggested Larry. "You tell me if you can handle it. No obligation, friend. If you'd as lief stay out of it, we'll understand."

"And—if I deliver this here message?" prodded Ike.

"Twenty bucks," said Larry. "In advance."

"Just for sayin' a few words in the Rialto?" Ike Bosely bared his surviving teeth in a wide grin. "Mister, you got yourself a messenger."

Toward noon, when the shabby loner ambled into the Rialto, Bonner and Marco were sharing a corner table with Mayor Garbutt and Cleat Dumont, the poker dealer. They paid little attention to Ike Bosely, who breasted the bar, paid in advance for a double shot of rye and began his spiel.

The barkeep was soon hanging on the old man's every word, urging him to expand. Ike played his role like an old professional from a tent show.

"Dunno who they are—and don't care," he mumbled. "All I know is the women are wailin' and three of them jaspers is shot up bad. Was a time when I had Nueva Fortuna all to myself, and that's how I like it. I don't crave company. Hell, I didn't invite them folks to move in. Guess I'll stay in town a couple days. I ain't goin' back till they've found someplace else to roost."

A few moments later, the prospector bought

and paid for a refill and toted it across to the roulette table to watch the play. The barkeep promptly signaled a houseman to fill in for him and sidled to the corner to talk to his boss.

Bonner listened intently, while Garbutt sweated and fretted and mopped at his brow, and Marco kept his haunted eyes on his drink.

"By Judas, it's perfect!" The saloonkeeper chuckled softly. "It *has* to be them!"

"Well," frowned the barkeep, "if the short one called the other one Floyd . . ."

"Their bodyguards badly wounded," grinned Bonner. "Floyd too. The only one still on his feet is that greedy, sawn-off blackmailer."

"Sonofabitch," sneered Dumont.

"So Mathews did what we paid him to do," Marco said softly. "And where is he now? The way it sounds to me, they set up an ambush— and Mike is the only survivor."

"Don't worry, Whit," drawled Bonner. "He won't survive much longer. We're about to finish it—once and for all."

"The Rigg sisters . . ." began Marco.

"Why in blazes didn't they head straight for Double R?" wondered Garbutt.

"Who cares?" shrugged Bonner. "Maybe

their horses were winded by the time they sighted Nueva Fortuna."

"And Floyd and those Texans were too weak to travel any further," grinned Dumont.

"You know what to do, Whit," Bonner said briskly. "Have our horses saddled and fetched to the back alley, and run across to the emporium. McMurtrie and Rusk have a stake in this." He nodded to Garbutt. "You too, Al."

"No—no—I couldn't," mumbled Garbutt. "Oh, hell! Those Rigg girls . . ."

"Can't afford to let the kid live," growled Bonner. "And we won't be leaving any witnesses. That's the way it has to be." He grinned sardonically as he rose to his feet. "But you stay here—if you have no stomach for it." He frowned at Marco. "What're you waiting for?"

"All right . . ." Marco nodded resignedly, rose and turned toward the entrance. "All right."

"I'll take Farley along," Bonner told Dumont. "You stay here, Cleat. I want you to keep an eye on Bosely. We don't want the old buzzard running to Doc Mulligan or the marshal, do we?"

"Give him a bottle and he'll stay till you want him thrown out," shrugged Dumont.

The old man hovered on the fringe of the players gathered about the roulette table, pretending not to notice the departure of Drake Bonner and Shotgun Farley, the latter hefting his formidable weapon and grinning in eager anticipation. He cocked an ear to the sounds in the rear alley—five riders—hoofbeats steadily receding. Dumont ambled toward him then, grinning blandly, toting a bottle, and Ike wondered if he was any match for the pomaded dandy. He dropped a gnarled paw into the right pocket of his baggy jacket and, by the time Dumont reached him, had withdrawn the hand again, the brown fingers concealing a tiny weapon of which Dumont was unaware until he stood beside him and began his invitation.

"Compliments of the house, old timer. Drake wants you should make yourself comfortable and . . ."

The gambler's voice choked off. Ike had lifted an arm as though to wrap it about his shoulders, but now his hand was rammed against Dumont's right kidney.

"Ain't much of a weapon, I guess," the prospector said softly. "One of them itty-bitty

222

derringers. A feller traded it to me for a few cans of beans. It's loaded, tinhorn, and it's cocked. Mightn't kill you—but I figure one of them snub-nosed slugs'd give you hell."

"What the . . . ?"

"Don't holler, and don't try signalin' the barkeep. Just keep your paws where I can see 'em and start walkin'."

"Listen, you crazy old coyote . . . !"

"Move out, tinhorn. I'm keepin' this thing poked tight agin you till we're in the marshal's office."

The gambler, irate but intimidated, moved across to the batwings with Ike never more than six inches away and the business-end of the derringer jabbing hard, harrowing proof that the old man wasn't fooling.

Jeb Noad and his father-in-law eyed them uncertainly when, a few moments later, they entered the law office. Dumont immediately began cursing the old man, but Ike prodded harder with his derringer and cut him short.

"Not another yap outa you. Mister Jailer, I'll thank you to relieve this galoot of his handgun. He's just bound to have some kinda shooter hid away."

Orin Platt took possession of Dumont's

shoulder-holstered .38 and the whiskey bottle. Ike then ordered the gambler to face the rear wall with his hands up, and proceeded to tell Noad a thing or two.

"I'm advisin' you to throw this dude in your calaboose and take yourself to Nueva Fortuna just as fast as a horse can tote you, Marshal. Feller name of Larry Valentine paid me twenty dollars to deliver a message." He went on to report the arrival of the Riggs and their bodyguards and his conversation with the Texans, and added an opinion. "Gonna be a showdown out there—and a whole mess of shootin'."

"Let me—get this straight," muttered Noad. "Bonner took four men out there—and you believe he means to kill Mike Rigg?"

"That's how Valentine figures it, and he's likely right," said Ike.

"He's lying!" raged Dumont. "He's loco!"

"Orin," said Noad, as he slowly rose from his chair, "I'll cover you while you stow Dumont in a cell. When I leave, I want you to keep the office door locked. And you arm yourself with a shotgun and sit guard by the window."

"If it's all the same to you, I'll hang around," said Ike, his thoughtful gaze on the whiskey bottle. "I got noplace special to go anyway."

Within five minutes of Dumont's arrest, Marshal Noad was riding fast out of San Jose, bound for the ghost town and urging his mount to its utmost speed, but grimly resigned to the prospect of reaching Nueva Fortuna too late to prevent bloodshed.

Stretch sighted the five riders in the early afternoon from his lofty vantagepoint, the roof of the old Posada Gomez, the ghost town's tallest surviving structure. Unhurriedly, he descended to the street and sauntered across to the saloon. The horses were still tethered to the hitch-rail out front; the stalled buckboard had been transferred to the alley beside the saloon. Inside, Floyd was pacing restlessly. Mike was feigning boredom, sitting near the bar, playing solitaire, while his sisters conversed in undertones and watched Larry, who was rummaging behind the bar in a vain search for a bottle.

From the doorway, Stretch reported, "They're comin' now."

The sisters tensed. Floyd jerked to an abrupt halt. Mike proved he wasn't bored by starting nervously and dropping his cards. Larry nodded impatiently, drew his Colt and checked its loading.

"How many?" he asked. "And how far off?"

"Five," said Stretch. "Comin' from San Jose, I'd say. About a mile off."

"That gives us all the time we need," muttered Larry. "All right, you Riggs. I already told you what you have to do. Don't make me say it all again."

"It ain't right for you and Stretch to take all the risks," Floyd protested.

"I ought to be in this hassle," insisted Mike. "Hell, Larry, I'm the one they want."

"You young bucks got a couple good-lookin' sisters," Larry gruffly reminded them. "If this is Bonner and his pards—and I don't know who else it could be—they're plannin' on shuttin' your mouth for keeps . . ."

"And leavin' no witnesses," drawled Stretch. "Beggin' your pardon, ladies, but that means you."

"You got an obligation, boys," declared Larry. "Like I said before, your job is to stay with your sisters, cover 'em, be ready to protect 'em if any of Bonner's sidekicks get past us."

"Just leave these jaspers to Larry and me," advised Stretch.

"Get goin' now," ordered Larry. "You know where. And remember—stay hid."

226

Belle and Nora walked to the entrance. The elder sister glanced sidelong at the Texans, her expression more eloquent than any carefully composed speech. Nora offered them a hesitant smile, then frowned impatiently at her brothers.

"Larry's right," Floyd said quietly. "We have to be sure about Belle and Nora."

From the saloon, the brothers escorted their sisters to the building nominated by Larry, the crumbling adobe shell of the Leggett & Binns Funeral Parlor half-way along the next block— the last place Bonner and his men would expect to find them.

Stretch led the horses into the side alley, then rejoined his partner on the saloon porch. Larry had improvised a barricade—a few pieces of broken furniture toted from the barroom. With his brown fingers busy with the building of a cigarette, he nonchalantly remarked,

"I don't aim to get in the way of your lead, runt. So I sure ain't stashin' myself right opposite of here."

"Right opposite'd be okay," shrugged Larry. "But get high."

"Roof across there." Stretch lit his cigarette and gestured to the ruin of the assay office. "As good a stakeout as any."

"Good enough," nodded Larry. "Take care, huh?"

"You too," grunted Stretch. "I guess, by sundown, we'll be deliverin' the young'uns to Double R."

"And a bunch of killers to the San Jose calaboose," growled Larry.

"Be seein' you," drawled the taller Texan.

He ambled across the street and along to the assay office. Minutes later, he was in position, sprawled on the roof and waiting patiently, and Larry was hunkered behind his barricade, cocking an ear for the sound of hoofbeats and glancing to either end of the street.

Drake Bonner's party came on boldly, all but Marco, who brought up the rear, haggard and apprehensive, slumped in his saddle. Riding stirrup to stirrup with his boss as they moved into the street, Farley grinned and cocked his shotgun and stared eagerly to left and right. Behind them, McMurtrie and Rusk brandished pistols and stared toward the alley north of the saloon.

"Horses over there," McMurtrie observed.

"I see them," nodded Bonner. "We might've guessed they'd shack up in the old Lodestar Bar. The only building with four whole walls."

Grinning, he drew rein. The others followed his example and, now, the five rogues were bunched, sitting their mounts some 25 yards from the saloon in plain sight of the Texans. "Let's get it over with," he drawled. "Call him out, McMurtrie."

"Rigg!" yelled McMurtrie. "Mike Rigg! Come on out!"

"No use hidin', kid!" boomed Farley. "You know we'll roust you out—so you might's well show yourself right now!"

"Listen to me, Rigg!" shouted Bonner. "This is Drake Bonner, and I'm here to talk a deal! I know Floyd's wounded—those saddletramps too! I brought Marco along, and he's a fair hand at doctoring! You gonna show yourself—or will you let your wounded bleed to death while we're looking for you?" Confidently, he assured his followers, "That'll fetch him."

Silence.

Marco fidgeted uneasily. McMurtrie and Rusk traded puzzled frowns, and then Bonner growled a command to Farley.

"Move on to the saloon. Let 'em have one charge of buckshot through the front wall. I've had my fill of waiting."

"It'll be a pleasure," grinned Farley.

He urged his mount forward. Larry waited until he had almost reached the porch, then showed himself, rising up with his Colt leveled.

"You with the cannon!" he called harshly. "Drop it—and grab sky!" As Farley jerked his mount to a slithering halt, he added another challenge, this time to the others. "That goes for all of you! Drop the hardware! You're covered!"

"He ain't wounded, damnitall!" raged Rusk. "We been tricked!"

Farley loosed an oath as his trigger-finger contracted, and Larry promptly dropped flat. The shotgun roared and buckshot riddled his makeshift barricade, as he rolled away from it. He reached the top of the stairs and, from a half-kneeling position, saw Farley charge forward, leveling his weapon again, and Bonner hastily emptying his holster, McMurtrie and Rusk swinging their mounts toward the far side-walk, Marco wheeling his animal and firing over his shoulder. Two .45 slugs came Larry's way, gouging chunks off the porch-rail. But, right now, he had to concentrate on the man with the shotgun. Farley was less than seven yards away, dipping the barrels to trigger his second charge, when Larry took aim and fired. The shotgun roared again, but with its muzzles pointed to the sky and Farley still gripping it, back-somersaulting off his horse with his chest bloody.

From his elevated vantagepoint, Stretch bellowed a command which McMurtrie and Rusk ignored. They had almost reached the opposite sidewalk, and now their guns were raised and booming. A bullet missed Stretch's head by inches. Another thudded into the roof directly below his position, as he opened fire, his matched Colts roaring in angry challenge. McMurtrie yelled and pitched to the dust. Rusk followed him, cursing wildly, falling on all fours and then beginning a frantic search for his pistol.

Bonner's gun barked and Larry gave him no chance for a second shot. His Colt roared again and another saddle was abruptly emptied; the saloonkeeper sprawled in the dust, his sightless eyes turned to the sky.

Marco was well-clear of the scene of carnage, spurring his mount to a gallop, when Stretch squinted along the barrel of his righthand Colt and triggered the last shot. His slug creased Marco's shoulder and the impact was too much for the ashen-faced gambler. Buffeted as though by a giant's hand, shoved off-balance, he made a grab for his saddlehorn, missed and crashed to the ground.

Stretch dropped from the roof and strode to the wounded storekeepers to pick up their guns. Rusk called him a name, tried to rise but couldn't make it. McMurtrie, sick with pain and fear, lay on his left side, his right hand clamped to the bullet-gash at his ribs, his face contorted.

Moving past the bodies of Farley and Bonner, Larry hustled to the end of the street to check on Marco. By the time Marshal Noad arrived, the Riggs were joining the Texans in the saloon. The dead lay where they had fallen. McMurtrie and Rusk were huddled by the bar, groaning from the agony of their wounds, and Marco was just regaining consciousness.

"What brings you out here?" Stretch mildly enquired, as the lawman hurried in.

"Bosely did more than deliver your message," frowned Noad. "He talked to me as well. Valentine, you got some explaining to do."

"Well, it's this way, Marshal . . ." began Mike.

"Let this jasper talk first," suggested Larry,

as he raised Marco to a sitting position. "Seems to me he's mighty eager."

"While my strength lasts . . ." Marco said huskily, "and while I can find the courage—to confess—to be rid of my guilt." Noad and the Rigg brothers crouched beside him, and he talked on. "I knew it couldn't stay buried—forgotten . . ."

"Keep it short and simple, mister," advised Larry.

"Joe Kyle . . ." Marco's eyes watered as he mouthed that name. "Drake and me—knew he'd hit it rich. We took his gold to our claim—after Drake killed him. And I—I held the old man—while Drake knifed him. Couldn't forget—the look in Kyle's eyes. He twisted and—looked into my face—just before he died . . ."

"Are we gonna lie here and bleed . . . ?" wailed Rusk.

"Shuddup!" snapped Larry.

"I don't know how—Mike Rigg learned our secret," mumbled Marco. "He was blackmailing us. All of us."

"All . . . ?" frowned Noad.

"McMurtrie and Rusk—and the mayor." In faltering sentences, Marco told of their deal with the Mathews gang, the conspiracy to murder Mike Rigg, and their motives. Mc-Murtrie gasped abuse, but the pain-wracked gambler could not be silenced. And then, in the moment before he lost consciousness again, he confided, "I'd have had to confess anyway. I'd gotten to where—I couldn't live with it any more."

The sisters were improvising bandages from strips torn from their petticoats. Floyd lent a hand, as they began doctoring the wounded men. Noad, recovering from his confusion, fixed a grim frown on the younger brother.

"Yeah, I heard what he told you," growled Mike. "And I'm bettin' it's all true. So now we know how Bonner got rich enough to start the Rialto, and how McMurtrie and his buddy set 'emselves up as storekeepers. And, doggone it, *everybody* knows about Mayor Garbutt and the Hewlett woman."

"Everybody but Lena Garbutt," muttered Noad.

"But one part of it *ain't* true," asserted Mike. "I didn't know a dad-blamed thing about how Joe Kyle disappeared, and I sure didn't know about that stagecoach robbery. Hell, Marshal, I never blackmailed these buzzards!"

"Marco said they got letters," mused Noad.

"Maybe you'll find some of those letters when you search Bonner's office—if he was fool enough to keep 'em," drawled Larry. "I'd say Mike can easily prove he didn't write 'em. All you have to do is check his fist against the blackmail notes. Plain enough, Marshal. There was a blackmailer, sure. But the blackmailer wasn't Mike."

"Some smart hombre that used his name," opined Stretch.

The taller Texan was intrigued by the irony of the situation. Whit Marco's confession was unexpected—and a reprieve for Sammy Carr, the real blackmailer, whose written confession was now cancelled out.

"Better be satisfied with what you've got," advised Larry.

"I got to admit it's hard for me to believe," conceded Noad. "Kyle dropped out of sight a long time back—about the time the stage was robbed. Mike was a lot younger then. Yeah, it's hard for me to believe."

"You've got Marco's confession," Larry pointed out. "And three wounded prisoners."

"And a reason for arresting Garbutt," said Noad, his eyes gleaming. "There's a name for

235

his crime. It's called conspiracy to murder. He's an accessory. And, by thunder, he'll be behind bars before this day is through."

The marshal of San Jose left Nueva Fortuna a half-hour later, traveling slowly, leading five horses, two of them carrying the blanket-wrapped bodies of Bonner and Farley, the other three straddled by Marco, McMurtrie and Rusk, barely conscious, their feet lashed to their stirrups to prevent their falling.

At about the same time that Larry and Stretch were leading the Riggs across Double R range, Noad was locking a cell-door on a blustering but defeated Al Garbutt, and the citizens were viewing their marshal with increased respect. The Bonner influence was suddenly as dead as Bonner himself and the Rialto had closed its doors. Garbutt's mistress and the other employees were beating a hurried retreat.

The Texans stayed mounted, trading weary grins, as the retrieved runaways and their parents held a joyful and noisy reunion on the porch of the Double R ranch-house. The sisters embraced Chloe, while Robbie grinned his amiable grin and traded handshakes and back-slaps with his whooping sons. Mike whisked his mother off her feet and yelled to Larry,

"Here she is—the purtiest Rigg of all!"

"And Robbie's the handsomest," Larry good-humoredly remarked.

"Land sakes, how they've grown!" gasped Chloe.

"Just as long as they ain't growed away from us," said Robbie.

"*That'll* be the day," chuckled Belle.

With her face pressed to her father's chest, Nora fervently vowed,

"We'll never wander again. We're home to stay."

"The Rigg family—all together—just like we wanted," Robbie bragged to his spouse. "Feels good, huh Chloe?"

"I got some prayin' to do," murmured Chloe, gazing wistfully at the Texans. "Been prayin' the Lord to send our young'uns home, and He heard me. And now I'll be thankin' Him—and you."

"Light and set," Robbie invited them. "Cool them saddles. Doggone it, we're celebratin', and . . ."

"Thanks just the same, old timer," drawled Larry. "You waited a long time for this get-together, and it ought to be strictly family."

"'Scuse us. We'll be movin' on now," said Stretch.

"Ten o'clock tomorrow mornin'," said Robbie. "Ten o'clock sharp, I'll be in town. You meet me at the bank, and I'll settle up with you."

"Yeah, sure," nodded Larry.

"Be seein' you," nodded Stretch.

They shook hands with Robbie and his sons, submitted to being kissed by Belle and Nora and their mother, then wheeled their mounts and rode away toward the San Jose. But, out of sight of the ranch-house, they detoured, heading east toward the Rio Grande.

Tomorrow, Robbie Rigg would wait in vain for them in San Jose. Full payment for the chore of rounding up the runaways would mean financial stability, a degree of affluence to which they were unaccustomed. They had cash—enough to keep a couple of fiddle-footed nomads eating regularly. They had undertaken a task, faced a crisis or two and risked their Texan hides to bring four redheads home unscathed. And now they would relax.

Until the next ruckus.

FARGO: MASSACRE RIVER
by John Benteen

Fargo spurred his horse to the edge of the road. The ambushers up ahead had now blocked the road. Fargo's convoy was a jumble, a perfect target for the insurgents' weapons!

SUNDANCE:
DEATH IN THE LAVA
by John Benteen

The land echoed with the thundering hoofs of Modoc ponies. In minutes they swooped down and captured the wagon train and its cargo of gold. But now the halfbreed they called Sundance was going after it, and he swore nothing would stand in his way.

GUNS OF FURY
by Ernest Haycox

Dane Starr, alias Dan Smith, wanted to close the door on his past and hang up his guns, but people wouldn't let him. Good men wanted him to settle their scores for them. Bad men thought they were faster and itched to prove it. Starr had to keep killing just to stay alive.

FARGO: PANAMA GOLD
by John Benteen

Cleve Buckner was recruiting an army of killers, gunmen and deserters from all over Central America. With foreign money behind him, Buckner was going to destroy the Panama Canal before it could be completed. Fargo's job was to stop Buckner—and to eliminate him once and for all!

FARGO: THE SHARPSHOOTERS
by John Benteen

The Canfield clan, thirty strong, were raising hell in Texas. One of them had shot a Texas Ranger, and the Rangers had to bring in the killer. Fargo was tough enough to hold his own against the whole clan.

SUNDANCE: OVERKILL
by John Benteen

Sundance's reputation as a fighting man had spread. There was no job too tough for the halfbreed to handle. So when a wealthy banker's daughter was kidnapped by the Cheyenne, he offered Sundance $10,000 to rescue the girl.

HELL RIDERS
by Steve Mensing

Wade Walker's kid brother, Duane, was locked up in the Silver City jail facing a rope at dawn. Wade was a ruthless outlaw, but he was smart, and he had vowed to have his brother out of jail before morning!

DESERT OF THE DAMNED
by Nelson Nye

The law was after him for the murder of a marshal—a murder he didn't commit. Breen was after him for revenge—and Breen wouldn't stop at anything . . . blackmail, a frameup . . . or murder.

DAY OF THE COMANCHEROS
by Steven C. Lawrence

Their very name struck terror into men's hearts—the Comancheros, a savage army of cutthroats who swept across Texas, leaving behind a bloodstained trail of robbery and murder.

SUNDANCE: SILENT ENEMY
by John Benteen

Both the Indians and the U.S. Cavalry were being victimized. A lone crazed Cheyenne was on a personal war path against both sides. They needed to pit one man against one crazed Indian. That man was Sundance.

LASSITER
by Jack Slade

Lassiter wasn't the kind of man to listen to reason. Cross him once and he'd hold a grudge for years to come—if he let you live that long. But he was no crueler than the men he had killed, and he had never killed a man who didn't need killing.

LAST STAGE TO GOMORRAH
by Barry Cord

Jeff Carter, tough ex-riverboat gambler, now had himself a horse ranch that kept him free from gunfights and card games. Until Sturvesant of Wells Fargo showed up. Jeff owed him a favour and Sturvesant wanted it paid up. All he had to do was to go to Gomorrah and recover a quarter of a million dollars stolen from a stagecoach!

McALLISTER ON THE COMANCHE CROSSING
by Matt Chisholm

The Comanche, deadly warriors and the finest horsemen in the world, reckon McAllister owes them a life—and the trail is soaked with the blood of the men who had tried to outrun them before.

QUICK-TRIGGER COUNTRY
by Clem Colt

Turkey Red hooked up with Curly Bill Graham's outlaw crew and soon made a name for himself. But wholesale murder was out of Turk's line, so when range war flared he bucked the whole border gang alone . . .

PISTOL LAW
by Paul Evan Lehman

Lance Jones came back to Mustang for just one thing—Revenge! Revenge on the people who had him thrown in jail; on the crooked marshal; on the human vulture who had already taken over the town. Now it was Lance's turn . . .